Why fight the

Remy Goes

Shara Az

He's playing you, Regina, she told herself. *This is little more than a game to him.* It might have been a game to him, but she was more than willing to play—for a little while anyway. A couple of days, max, and he would move on. He had to; Regina couldn't afford to let it last much more than that. Most of all, she needed to be sure she guarded her heart. Nothing good could come from falling for Remy Chevalier.

Regina entered the kitchen more calmly than she'd left. Noting he had pulled a chair from the table, she sank into the seat to watch Remy work his magic at her stove. It was odd to watch him cook. He seemed completely comfortable, moving around the kitchen like a pro. She was surprised, but then again, she didn't know all that much about him. She remembered Angelique commenting that Remy often cooked for her and Thierry, but Regina had never given it more than a passing thought.

"Here," Remy told her, handing her a glass of wine with a wink. "I stole a couple of bottles from Thierry and Angel."

Regina took it. After a couple of sips, she couldn't resist asking. "Why are you here, really?"

Remy sighed and turned to face her. He couldn't tell her the real reason: He couldn't stay away. He tried to, but every thought led right back to her. He loved being able to get under her skin a little bit, to ruffle her feathers. Regina was always so damn composed, it drove him crazy. He had not expected the dynamo in bed; but that made her all the more irresistible.

Cacoethes Books are published by

Cacoethes Publishing House, LLC.
14715 Pacific Avenue South
Suite 604
Tacoma, WA 98444

All Cacoethes titles imprints and distributed lines are available at special quantity discounts for bulk purchases for sales promotion, premiums, fund-raising, educational or institutional use.

Special book excerpts or customized printings can also be created to fit specific needs. For details, write or phone the office of the Cacoethes Sales Manager:

Cacoethes Publishing House, LLC.
14715 Pacific Avenue South, Suite 604
Tacoma, WA 98444.
Attn. Sales Department.
Phone: 253-536-3747
ISBN:

Printed in the United States of America

Cacoethes Publishing House, LLC.
14715 Pacific Avenue South
Suite 604
Tacoma, WA 98444

Remy Goes to Therapy
Copyright © 2008 by Shara Azod
Cover by PK1 Studios
ISBN: 00013
Ebook ISBN: 00013
www.cacoëthespublishing.com

REMY GOES TO THERAPY

SHARA AZOD

"There is always some madness in love.
But there is also always some reason in madness."
~Friedrich Nietzsche

CHAPTER ONE

Remy retreated to the back of the ballroom, undoing his tie and discarding it in the nearest potted plant. As happy as he was for his cousin Thierry and his new wife Angelique, he felt a strange sense of melancholy sweep over him. Thierry had been the first to succumb to Cupid's arrow, but by the looks of things he wouldn't be the last. Remy's twin, Rance, had it bad for Angelique's friend Jade, though he was trying like hell not to show it. While it had been fun to hassle Thierry about his obsession with his wife, Rance would just be a buzz-kill. The man simply couldn't take a joke. As far as he knew, his twin didn't even have a sense of humor.

Safely hidden from view, Remy looked out at all the well-wishers. Well, only about half of this over-privileged crowd actually wished the couple well. The other half was appalled at the mixed-race marriage. Remy was delighted. Not just because it put several well-to-do noses out of joint, but also because Thierry deserved to be happy. Hell, all the Chevalier boys deserved to be happy. They'd had collectively miserable childhoods.

They'd been raised by their demon of a grandmother, and their respective mothers had all been systematically removed from their lives one way or another. Remy's mother had fared better than the other Chevalier wives: She'd died in childbirth. Thierry's mother had been deemed inappropriate because she was a Yankee and a little too liberal in her views. Kind of the way Mussolini was a little too liberal for Hitler. That marriage lasted long enough to see Thierry's father, Beaumont, well on his way to a successful political career, then the woman disappeared north, never to be seen or heard from again. She apparently died when Thierry was ten.

Aubrey's mother, bless her soul, had literally withered away. She never had a say in her child's life, and her husband was far too busy to be bothered with her after she had produced the requisite Chevalier progeny; she spent most of her days alone in her rooms until she eventually withered away to nothing. Remy secretly suspected that Lady Rienne, his grandmother and matriarch of the family, had poisoned her. There was no way to prove it, so he decided to let that one go. No one was really sure what happened to Piers' mother. She was there one day, gone the next. It was amazing to see a grown woman disappear and no one comment on it. It was almost as if she never existed.

Shaking off his morose thoughts, Remy continued scanning the crowd. He was determined to find someone interesting to talk to. Okay, honestly he was looking for either someone to torment, or someone to fuck. Either worked for him. He was just about to settle on torturing one of Lady Rienne's so-called "close friends" when he saw Angelique's other friend with the lawyer-chick Rance was crazy about. *Ah yes, the psychiatrist.*

Now there was a woman in serious need of some loosening up. She was dressed in a simple, conservative black Audrey Hepburn-style sheath dress complete with small, white pearl earbobs and necklace. By the way she moved, Remy could tell she had no idea how the dress hugged her hourglass figure and emphasized lush curves. She had an ass that made a man want to beg: Full, plentiful and firm. It looked firm anyway. He wished he could take an experimental squeeze just to be sure.

Remy watched the dark-skinned woman as she smiled and moved among the crowd. Her hair was still coiled in a tight bun. In fact, the few times he had seen her, her hair had been in that same damn bun. Everything about her seemed to be under complete control. *What would it be like to see her hair down? What would it be like to see all that cool control thrown right out the window? What kind of man would make her lose control?* His cock hardened precipitously at the thought. What he wouldn't give to be that man.

"That Remy is watching you again," Jade whispered in Regina's ear.

Despite playing cool and collected, Regina felt her panties moisten slightly at the thought of those wicked eyes watching her. He probably just wanted to talk. Once people found out her profession, they seemed to want to corner her at parties and "talk." Free therapy was more like it. While Remy Chevalier could certainly use some therapy, she wasn't volunteering to be the therapist. Still, a girl could fantasize, couldn't she? And with a bad boy like Remy, there was plenty to fantasize about.

However, bad boys were only good for fantasizing. She would be completely out of her element with anything else. Regina Booker never dated bad boys. She studied them, counseled them, and yes, even lusted and fantasized about them. But she never got involved with them. From what she could gather, they weren't worth the trouble. She only slept with men she was deeply involved with. She couldn't count how many times she'd been dumped because she wouldn't give it up until she was sure about the man she was with. A couple of dates wouldn't cut it for her.

Just by observing Remy in the few times she'd been around him, Regina could tell he was the love-'em-and-leave-'em type. Besides, he was white. She had nothing against interracial relationships; she just didn't do them. She would never date a man she couldn't bring home to her parents.

Though Regina had been raised in New York, her parents were both from the South. Her father had attended school the first year his small Georgia town had integrated the public schools. The experience had left an indelible scar. Reggie Booker was none too fond of white people in general, or white men in particular. For her to date one would be a betrayal of the man who had always been there for her. He and her mother had worked two jobs each to put her through LSU so she wouldn't have to take out thousands of dollars in loans.

"No child o'mine is going start out in life owing money," he had told her.

Nope, Remy was fine for her dreams, but better left alone in real life. She was about to tell Jade just that when a pair of very strong arms swung her around.

"Dance with me," Remy told her, not really giving her a chance to decline. Before Regina knew what was happening, she was in the middle of the dance floor, being whirled by Remy's very capable hands.

As much as she wanted to leave him right there on the floor, she wanted to stay even more. His hands were large and very warm. She could feel them through her dress every time he whirled and dipped her to the song the zydeco band was playing. Her heart sped just glancing at him; his loosely curled black hair looked windblown and carefree. Her hands actually itched to bury themselves in those silky curls. Once or twice, she dared to look into those perpetually laughing blue-green eyes. *Jeez, what was it with the Chevalier family and those damn blue-green eyes?* Remy's were framed by impossibly long jet-black lashes. He even had the audacity to have dimples. Dimples! Add that to a body that should be illegal to have and he was a walking, talking advertisement for sex. Long, hot, steamy sex. The kind that had you sweating out your perm.

One dance and I'm outta here, Regina said to herself. Her panties were now soaking wet. Remy was a temptation she just didn't need right now. It had been a long dry spell; she was probably just horny.

The up-tempo song ended, quickly replaced by smooth jazz. Sighing with relief, Regina began to move away, but found herself pressed against a hard, lean body instead.

"You weren't gonna run away, now were you, *cher*?"

Had his voice always been so sexy? His eyes sparkled with all kinds of mischief, the kind of mischief Regina probably didn't need.

"Look, Remy, you're a nice guy and all, but—"

"But you don't like the way I dance?" One hand held her wrist, but the other crept to the small of her back, swinging her in circles while keeping her pressed securely against him. "Too much rhythm," he sighed mournfully.

"What?"

"I have too much rhythm. It's a Louisiana-white-boy thing." She had been prepared for flirting, but now she found herself disarmed. She suddenly noticed that they were no longer in the middle of the dance floor. She felt the cool, hard wall against her back. There were two large

10

potted palms on either side of them, effectively blocking the view of any curious onlookers. *Uh-oh*, Regina thought to herself.

"Um, well, thanks for the dance," she said, trying to move to the side to squeeze around him.

Remy didn't move. He did let go of her wrist, placing his hand on the wall by her head. She could feel a very certain part of his anatomy growing against her stomach. Pressing her thighs together, she steeled herself, reaching for inner calm. *I will not give in; I will not leave this ballroom with him. I will be strong.* She was a professional psychiatrist, for crying out loud! Remy was a classic example of the narcissistic playboy. He wasn't really interested in her. He only seemed interested because she failed to respond to his constant flirting and sexual innuendos. She would never in a million years admit that she was interested or that the real reason she paid no attention to him was that he intrigued on a level that was far from clinical. It was a guilty secret best left buried deep in her psyche.

"I know what you're afraid of." Remy's voice deepened with restrained desire. He used his natural southern drawl for devastating effects. His words tended to wash over the skin in a smooth caress. Regina squirmed uncomfortably, trying to concentrate on anything but the way he made her want to melt.

"I am afraid you have mistaken me for someone else." She was inordinately proud of the way she sounded: Clear, concise and in complete control. It wouldn't do at all to let him know he was getting to her.

"I know exactly who you are, Dr. Regina Belle Booker."

Regina cringed. How the hell had he managed to find out her middle name? More importantly, why would he want to? *You're playing with the big boys now, Regina Belle.*

"What exactly do you want from me, Mr. Chevalier?" She used her best doctor-to-patient voice. The one that projected authority. It generally worked to cool off even the most amorous advances.

Remy frowned. He hadn't planned on backing her into the corner. He had only wanted to see her ruffled a little. He knew better than to try for anything more with Dr. Booker. She specialized in digging into a person's innermost thoughts, and he had skeletons best left dead and buried. He didn't want to let it go though. There was something about Regina that dared him. Just once, he needed to see her lose control a little. Or at least take down that damn bun.

"I want you to admit you're afraid," he told her, shifting so his growing erection rubbed against her even more. She ignored it.

"Afraid of what, exactly?"

She sounded exasperated. Good. At least now she was showing some kind of reaction. Not really the emotion he was looking for, but for some reason he needed this woman to respond to him.

"You're afraid I might be too, uh, *much* for you to handle," he smirked.

If you only knew, Regina thought. "Excuse me?"

"You know, the white man, big... attribute thing," Remy replied with a perfectly straight face. "You don't have to worry, *cher*. I know it might be somewhat larger than average, but I swear, I'll be real careful."

12

Regina didn't know whether to laugh or cry. She could definitely *feel* that he was working with quite a bit. Just the thought of it had her growing wetter by the second. She had to get away from him before she did something she knew she would regret.

Remy smiled as he watched her flounder for something to say. Finally! He was beginning to think she wasn't attracted to him. He knew damn well she felt his now-throbbing cock pushed against her. Unable to resist, he leaned down to give her a little peck on the cheek. Regina had chosen that moment to turn her head, expecting him to go for the lips. A whisper of a touch, flesh barely meeting, was all it took.

"Ah, hell," Remy muttered. He went in for the kill.

Before he could stop himself, he had one hand taking down the offensive bun, the other holding her by the hip as he plundered that sweet, sexy mouth. She tasted like fruit and wine, his favorite combination. Moving her dress up her hips, her explored a little, finding that she was wearing a thong. When he lifted her so he could press against her more intimately, he felt the wetness escaping from what felt like silk. God, how he wanted to rip the damn clothes right off her! He swallowed her soft little cries as he moved his fingers closer to her heated little pussy. Tight and wet, the very best kind.

Tearing his mouth away, he looked down. A thong of red silk. Dropping to his knees, he drew the panties down, helping her step out of them before burying his head right in her crotch.

Regina bit her lip to keep from crying out. Casting a quick glance around, she tried to move away. Regina Booker did *not* let men go down on her in a crowded ballroom! Remy had her hips firmly grasped in his hands as he burrowed his way between her legs. With the first flick of his tongue, Regina gave up trying to get away. He ran his tongue back and forth, lightly touching her clit. When he felt her relax, he moved one hand to expose the delicate little button and swirled his tongue around it, licking as if it were his favorite flavor lollypop. He dipped down to push his tongue deep inside her, then went back to lavish more attention on her needy little clit, this time alternating licking and sucking, while placing two fingers deep inside her. She tried to hold back, but it was too much. She came like a rocket, biting her lip so hard she tasted blood.

Remy rocked back on his knees, looking up at a now *very* ruffled Regina. Her soft black hair fell to the top of her shoulders and her chest heaved as she tried to catch her breath. Her deep brown eyes held the tell-tale glaze of a woman who had just been pleasured. He hadn't meant for it to go that far, but he was far from sorry. His own chest swelled in pride at the factthat he had finally made Regina Belle lose control. Damn but she looked beautiful leaning against the wall, her legs spread slightly. He wanted more.

Smoothing her dress down, Remy pocketed the panties and hair band, rose to his feet, and grabbed her hand.

"Come on, Regina Belle." If he gave her time to think about it he knew she would balk. He had to get her home and into his bed before he did something he would regret.

CHAPTER TWO

Regina couldn't say she didn't have a chance to back out and hightail it home. Even as Remy grabbed her by the elbow and practically dragged her out of the reception, she could have stopped him if she'd really wanted to. Truth was, she wanted to see how it would end. There could never be anything other than this one night. not that Remy was the type to offer anything more. She noticed curious glances in their direction as he whisked her out into the lobby and then into the back of a waiting limousine. She didn't even have a chance to sit down, instead, she found her dress at her waist again, her legs straddling his firm thighs. She marveled at how savagely beautiful he looked in the dim light. Men weren't supposed to be beautiful, but Remy was. Not feminine—he was utterly and completely masculine. But there was an exquisiteness to him that could only be described as sheer male beauty.

"Sorry sweetheart, I just can't wait."

Regina wondered what he was talking about, until she felt it. With one masterful upward stroke, he completely buried every vainglorious inch as deep as he could possibly go. Her breath escaped in a rushing gasp. Dear God, he hadn't been lying! The man was huge! He stretched her seldom-used pussy just to the point of pain, but it was just too delicious to stop.

"Don't move," Remy ordered. He eased her little black dress down her arms, but refused to pull her out of the garment completely. Instead, he grabbed both her hands with one of his own and held them behind her back. The other hand palmed her ass, pressing her down ruthlessly on his marauding cock as he pistoned upward in short, brutal strokes. Arching backward, Regina's thighs gripped his as she pushed her body down and his hips rose. Remy felt his cock grow even harder inside her as he watched the play of both pleasure and pain cross her face. Her breasts taunted him insolently, begging to be played with. Not one to decline such a tasty invitation, he bit down lightly on one blackberry-colored nipple before sucking it into his mouth, then turned his head to treat the other. As soon as his teeth lightly grazed the second nipple, he felt her vaginal walls contract, suckling his cock like a tight greedy little mouth.

"Fuck!" Remy ground his teeth as he fought to hold out, but it was too late. The spasms contracting tightly against his turgid length were too much. He came with her, grinding upwards in a desperate attempt to get as deep inside her as possible.

It was not enough. Even as they lay slumped together in the back seat, Remy wanted more. His erection hadn't dissipated, but was still impossibly hard and buried inside her. He hadn't really meant to take her yet. It was her ass that did it. As she climbed into the back of the car, he'd stared at her beautiful backside and lost what little control he had left. Lord knows he'd wanted to take her against the wall in the ballroom. Truth be told, he was proud that he'd persevered long enough to at least make it out of the reception. Regina Belle was not a snack to be gobbled quickly, she was a seven-course meal he had every intention of savoring. Thank God he had told to the driver to drop them off at Angelique's former home on Dauphine Street. It was too far for Regina to walk back to her place, private enough so no one would hear her screams (or his own), and no one would think to look for them there.

"Why are we here?" Regina asked, looking at the neighborhood in which they had stopped as she scrambled off his lap and tried to pull herself together.

His penis slipped from its warm cocoon with a slight sucking pop, but remained saluting as he tried to stuff it back in his pants. Forgetting trying to zip up the damn things, he simply pulled his dress shirt over it, causing it to tent out brazenly. Oh well. It was late; chances were no one would see it.

"You don't think we're done, do you, Regina Belle?"

Regina was saved from answering by the chauffeur, who opened the door and gave her a hand out of the vehicle. Fine, she would go inside and call a cab. She had no desire to argue with Remy, but she knew she shouldn't spend the night with him. His good looks and charm were dangerous enough, but what he'd just done to her in the back of the damn limo could have a woman hooked if she wasn't careful. Except she had absolutely no intention of becoming hooked on him.

He could guess at Regina's intention to leave as soon as possible, and as soon as he closed and locked the door, Remy snaked his arms around her, spinning her against the door.

"Put your hands on the door and don't move them," he growled in her ear as he pulled her rear against his over-eager member.

Regina didn't even think about it before she did it, then cursed mentally. She'd really had every intention of heading straight to the phone and calling a cab. She tried to turn around, but Remy was there, his front pressed against her back while his hands grasped her own, pinning her palms down against the door.

"Regina Belle, if you insist on being a bad girl, I'm going to have to spank that scrumptious ass of yours."

She couldn't suppress the tiny shiver that raced down her spine to the area in question. She had never been spanked, had never been with anyone that adventurous. Up until tonight, all of her experiences had been decidedly vanilla. Not bad, but not exactly something to shout about.

Remy smiled at the almost imperceptible reaction. Letting go of her hands, he eased the dress up until he reached her upper chest.

"Raise your arms."

She didn't even attempt to do anything else.

"Now put your hands back against the door," he commanded as soon as she was free of all clothing.

Taking a small step back, Remy ran his eyes up and down her form. Damn, she was hot! Her skin was downright flawless. He hadn't bothered to turn on the light, so he wasn't able to detect the reddish undertones he knew to be present in her truffle-colored complexion. Her legs weren't particularly long, but well-muscled, curving just right. Her waist dipped in from her torso only to flair out again, curving into the sweetest ass ever known to mankind. Delicious. He had to last this time. If not, he would just do it over and over until he got it right. He knew this would probably be his one and only night with her; he had to make it last.

"Spread your legs, baby," he whispered hoarsely, his hands going to cover his now-throbbing penis as she did so. God, the sight was so beautiful it could make a grown man cry. Or burst.

He had meant to take this one slow, he really had, but as he entered from behind, her pussy clamped down on him so tightly he couldn't stop his hips from slamming into her, back and forth, loving the muffled screams she was trying so hard to hold inside, the way her hands had curled into fists against the door, and most especially, the way her passage grew wetter and wetter with each stroke. Winding his right arm around her waist, he let his hand dip to caress her clit as he slammed into her harder and harder. The response was immediate.

"Oh, God, Remy! Yes!"

Regina's eyes crossed as a trail of explosions rocked her from inside out, each one more powerful than the last. And still he didn't stop. Every thrust of his hips hit just right, perfect in length and force. His wayward hand manipulated her to higher and higher heights, until she was almost positive her feet were no longer on the ground. She knew she was beginning to babble incoherently, but couldn't bring herself to care, much less stop. She, who had known nothing but quiet, pleasing orgasms, was screaming at the top of her lungs. She didn't know how much more she could take; her legs were literally shaking.

"Fuck!" Remy shouted as he came in a roaring rush. More. He had to have more. What was it about Regina Belle that made him need her again and again? He couldn't answer the question, and for tonight, he couldn't care less. He did know that he had to find a bed. He was a long way from being done.

*****

Regina yawned as she tried to concentrate on the notes in front of her. Remy had kept her up all night. If someone had told her yesterday she would spend the entire night having the most incredibly hot sex she'd ever experienced in her life, she would have laughed in their face. It wasn't until dawn broke that he finally fell asleep, and she had a chance to slip out of the house. She had just enough time to take a quick shower and change before coming in to the office. Still, she couldn't complain. She was deliciously sore in all the right places. Remy Chevalier was one serious sex machine. She had never dreamed that a woman could be pleasured so thoroughly.

"Dr. Booker, a new patient has called, asking for an appointment at three-thirty. Can you see him today, or would you like for me to schedule some other time?"

The sound of her secretary's voice broke her out of her daydream. Last night had been fun, but now it was back to the real world for Regina.

"I can take on a new patient today," Regina replied. It was best to stay as busy as possible. Maybe that way she could keep her mind off of Remy. She couldn't imagine anything good coming out of turning a one-night stand into something more than what it really was. He just wasn't long-term material.

The rest of the day went by reasonable quickly, though she had a hard time staying focused on her patients. The majority of people she saw were single adults who really didn't need a psychiatrist as much as they needed someone to listen. Generally, she would have a few sessions with them, then refer them to a therapist who specialized in people without any real psychoses. Her specialty was adults with *real* problems; some stemming from abusive childhoods, some from treatable diseases like schizophrenia or bipolar disorder. She preferred to deal with people with true medical conditions, but it usually took a few sessions to tell who really needed her help and who didn't. Occasionally she would get a patient just looking for prescription meds. It never ceased to amaze her how some people thought they could read up on some serious disorder and try to fake it in front of a professional.

By the time three-thirty rolled around, Regina was truly tired. Lack of sleep was catching up to her with a vengeance. After this session, she was heading straight home to bed. She wondered what time Remy had finally awakened. Was he disappointed that she had snuck out while he slept? Probably not. She was willing to bet he had plenty of one-night stands just like last night. She had never done anything like that before, nor would she again, but she didn't regret a single second.

"Dr. Booker, your three-thirty is here," the disembodied voice of her secretary informed her.

"Send him in," Regina told her, trying to shake off musings of last night. Shuffling through the papers on her desk, she failed to see the object of her thoughts walk in and silently close and lock the door.

"Well, Regina Belle, do you think you can help me?"

CHAPTER THREE

"What are you doing here?" Regina demanded. "This is my place of business, Remy; I don't have time to play with you."

Remy shrugged, completely unfazed by her anger. He was far more focused on the way her nipples pebbled underneath that prim silk shirt. Her hair was back in the damnable bun, but the day was young yet.

"What makes you think I'm playing?" he asked mischievously .

If looks could kill, he would surely be dead.

"I deal with people with real problems," Regina hissed between her teeth. "Your only problem is narcissism."

"Ouch!" Remy laughed; she was so cute when she was angry. The way her nostrils flared out a little and she clenched her jaw was kind of sexy. "As it so happens, I have many, many problems." *Wasn't that the truth!* "The first being a very sexy woman slipped out of my bed in the wee hours of the morning without a word. I woke cold and alone. Nearly broke my heart."

Regina took some deep, calming breaths. He was trying to rile her. She would not let that happen. There was only way to deal with someone like Remy. She could not let him see he was getting to her. Sitting behind her desk, she regarded him with cool detachment.

"One, it wasn't your bed," she informed him. "And two, because I have slept with you, I cannot possibly treat you for any of your so-called problems. It's not ethical."

"Sneaking out of bed is?"

He should have been grateful she'd left while he slept. It certainly ensured there would be no awkwardness. But for some reason, it had just pissed him off. He'd made the appointment with her secretary before he had a chance to think about what he was doing. There was just something about her. He couldn't seem to leave Regina alone—but he refused to think about the reasons behind his feelings.

"What do you want from me, Remy?" Regina asked tiredly. She wanted him to leave so she could go home and get some sleep.

Everything, he thought. "Therapy," he said out loud.

"Fine." Regina pulled out her notebook. He wanted to play, she would give him an hour. By the time she was done, he would never pull this crap again. "Tell me a little about what's bothering you."

"I told you. A beautiful woman snuck out on me." Remy was thoroughly enjoying himself. She may appear calm on the outside, but he was getting to her, he knew he was.

"So you have commitment issues," Regina responded, nonchalantly writing away on her notebook. "Do you think this stems from your parents' relationship, or was there something in your past that makes you afraid of commitment?"

"Since she was the one that ran out on me, don't you think it's her with the commitment issues?" he asked smugly. Regina was bound and determined to wipe that smirk right off his face.

"So, you were offering commitment?" She didn't need to look up to see that she had scored a point on that one.

"Uh, no," Remy squirmed a little in his seat. Damn, he should have seen that one coming. "Not right away, maybe. But the possibility was there."

"Are you looking for the possibility of commitment, then?"

"Uh, I…" Well, hell. Was he? "Maybe something more than a one-night stand, and see where it goes from there."

"So are you thinking maybe the possibility of moving in together—or, given one of the people closest to you has just gotten married, maybe you are thinking of finding someone you could spend the rest of your life with?"

"Hell no!" he shouted before he thought the better of it. "Never! Not me!"

Yeah, she thought so. Regina went on without missing a beat. "Again I ask, do you think this stems from your parents' relationship, or was there something in your past that makes you afraid of commitment? Have you been spurned by love?"

Okay, so maybe she was getting to him a bit too. "I never saw my parents together," he answered honestly, not at all sure why he did so. "And nothing happened in my past…"

He stopped so suddenly that Regina looked up from her notes. He had a stricken far-off look in his eyes that made her want to rush over to comfort him. Ruthlessly suppressing the urge, she waited patiently until he seemed to come back to the present.

"What makes you think I'm afraid of commitment?" He was trying to hold something in, but the sudden sadness in him made Regina want to reach out for him. It was too much to hope that he would actually share what had just gone through his mind. He didn't trust her yet. It generally took several sessions for someone to open up. Especially someone with trauma in their past. Whatever Remy had been thinking about had been tragic.

"When was the last time you were in a serious relationship?" Regina asked gently.

Remy had *never* been in a serious relationship. He couldn't put a woman through that, not after what had happened before. Memories rushed from the corners of his mind with an intense pain he hadn't allowed himself to feel in years. He had been so young, so naïve. So goddamn full of himself.

"This was a bad idea," Remy said, suddenly pushing himself to his feet. "I'll see you around."

And with that he was gone, leaving Regina to stare after him. She hadn't expected that. She'd always thought of Remy as the carefree playboy who'd never had any real problems in his life. Now she knew that wasn't the case. Whatever was really hiding behind his wisecracks and strings of casual encounters had hurt him deeply. He probably wasn't even aware that he was running from whatever tragedy he had experienced.

You will not get involved, Regina told herself as she gathered her purse and keys. She could not help Remy get over whatever he had gone through. He would have to want help first, and she might be a little too close to the subject to be objective. If he came back, she would refer him to someone else, but she seriously doubted he would return.

After informing her secretary she was going home for the day, she made a mental list of all the things she would do over the weekend. All her friends would be busy, so she would probably take the time to get some things done around the house. Maybe she would work in her garden. By the time she made it home, all she could think about was getting some sleep. Throwing her things on the living room couch, she undressed as she made her way to the bedroom, not bothering to change into her nightclothes as she fell onto the bed in her bra and panties. It wasn't like anyone would see anyway. She was asleep before her head even hit the pillow.

*****

Remy had no idea where he was going when he left Regina's office, he just knew he couldn't stay there. Though he hadn't said anything out loud, she had known something happened to him. Maybe she didn't know all the details, but she had seen deep into his pain. He couldn't allow her to see any more than that. He didn't think he could stand to see the disgust in her eyes if she ever knew. He was an idiot to ever try to play with her like this. He hadn't meant for it to happen, but he couldn't really say he was sorry for it. He just didn't know how to deal with all the feelings he'd thought were long since dead and buried. And she had seen pain lingering deep inside him.

What else could he expect, messing around with a psychiatrist? He just couldn't seem to help himself. He had believed one night would be enough, but when he woke to find her gone, he immediately wanted to see her again. He wanted her in a way he hadn't wanted anything, or anyone—ever. But he didn't deserve Regina Belle or the bliss he found in her arms. He wasn't good enough for a woman like that. Hell, he wasn't good enough for any woman. The problem was, he wanted her so badly, he knew he would never be able to stay away.

He'd thought he just wanted to see her loosen up a little. As soon as he got his first taste of her succulent lips, he knew he had to have her, just once. Now that he had, he wanted her again and again. Did she even know how damn good she felt? The way her silken sheath clamped down on his cock, her walls milking his very soul. Shit! This was not good. He had to get the woman out of his system. He didn't need this. There were plenty of woman out there who were more than willing to give him a little solace without taking a piece of his soul.

Several hours later, he found himself scowling at any woman daring to approach him at a respectable bar on Bourbon Street. He didn't want any other woman. He wanted Regina Belle Booker. It wouldn't last, it couldn't; but just for a little while, he wanted the sweet oblivion he found in her arms. He was tired. Tired of hanging out in bars and clubs with no real aim or purpose in life. He told himself that he lived the life he lived to get back at his grandmother, the infamous Lady Rienne. He was supposedly doing the exact opposite of what she'd planned for him. His carefully crafted persona was meant to thumb the nose at everything Lady Rienne embodied: Inherited wealth, Southern aristocracy, conservative values. In reality, he really was little more than a dissolute playboy with little aim and no real rhyme or reason.

It was terrifying that one night with a single woman could inspire such feelings. He would be better off staying as far away from her as possible. It would not end well. It couldn't. Regina was a decent woman, and he was far from being a decent man. He was no good for her. He couldn't bring anything of value to her life. So why was it that he found himself outside her front door with a bag full of groceries?

Regina groaned at the insistent ringing of her doorbell. She didn't want to get up, but whoever it was at her door wasn't going away. Cracking open one eye, than the other, she saw it was a little after nine o'clock in the evening. She had gotten home around four, so she had gotten about five hours of deep, undisturbed sleep. She still felt like she'd just gone about ten rounds in the boxing ring. Sluggishly, she rose to her feet, remembering halfway to the door she had nothing but her panties on. Damn! Looking back towards her bedroom, she decided against going back. It was probably just Katrina anyway.

Cracking open the door, she was totally unprepared for the man who pushed past her and into her home.

"What are you doing here?" Regina demanded as Remy pushed past her to stalk toward her kitchen.

Regina had a small home close to—but not exactly in—the French Quarter. Just a block away from her office, it was in a decent, working-class neighborhood. It was a two-bedroom, one-bath starter home. Perfect for a young, single professional. Most of her neighbors were a bit on the elderly side, which worked fine for her. They were always watching out for each other here. Unfortunately, that also meant her neighbors were a bit nosy. Generally, that didn't bother her. But then again, she had never had a man in her house before.

"As much as I appreciate you greeting me at the door in such a, uh, delightful outfit, I must insist you close the door, sweetheart." Remy smiled at her, his eyes glued to her chest.

With a muttered curse, Regina slammed the door, crossing her arms over her breasts.

"What are you doing here, Remy?' she demanded, refusing to run to her bedroom to cover herself. "And how did you know where I lived?"

"Asked Angel," he replied, busying himself with unpacking whatever he had in the bags. "And I'm making dinner."

Regina watched in confused fascination as he went about her kitchen like he lived there. It took a few minutes for her to remember she was standing there in her underwear. Stomping to her bedroom, she threw on some sweats, trying to calm her racing heartbeat. She should be pissed as hell at Remy's sudden arrival, but she almost wasn't. If anything, she was excited to see him. When he'd left her office earlier, she'd truly thought that it would be the end of their little interlude, and despite her better judgment, she was thrilled to see him. How could she not be? The man had done things to her she had never even read about.

He's playing you, Regina, she told herself. *This is little more than a game to him.* It might have been a game to him, but she was more than willing to play—or a little while anyway. A couple of days, max, and he would move on. He had to; Regina couldn't afford to let it last much more than that. Most of all, she needed to be sure she guarded her heart. Nothing good could come from falling for Remy Chevalier.

Regina entered the kitchen more calmly than she'd left. Noting he had pulled a chair from the table, she sank into the seat to watch Remy work his magic at her stove. It was odd to watch him cook. He seemed completely comfortable, moving around the kitchen like a pro. She was surprised, but then again, she didn't know all that much about him. She remembered Angelique commenting that Remy often cooked for her and Thierry, but Regina had never given it more than a passing thought.

"Here," Remy told her, handing her a glass of wine with a wink. "I stole a couple of bottles from Thierry and Angel."

Regina took it. After a couple of sips, she couldn't resist asking. "Why are you here, really?"

Remy sighed and turned to face her. He couldn't tell her the real reason: He couldn't stay away. He tried to, but every thought led right back to her. He loved being able to get under her skin a little bit, to ruffle her feathers. Regina was always so damn composed, it drove him crazy. He had not expected the dynamo in bed; but that made her all the more irresistible.

"It's your ass," he told her.

Regina choked on the wine she was swallowing. "What?"

Remy came over and kneeled in front of where she was sitting, looked her dead in the eye, and said with all seriousness, "Your ass, Regina Belle. It haunts me. I can't get it out of my mind. It's just so beautiful—high, round, and firm. It is so perfect. It calls to me, baby. I had to come."

CHAPTER FOUR

Dinner had been delicious; Remy really was a master chef. Lounging around her living room, Regina found it hard to see him as the ne'er-do-well lady's man she had always thought he was. After dinner, he had rubbed her feet as he plied her with wine and stories about his childhood with his brother and three cousins. She wondered idly whether he was even aware of all that he had revealed to her. Now, sitting alone in her office, she viewed him through the eyes of professional therapist. He had wanted to make her happy, to prove to her that he was more than hot sex and funny wisecracks. For some reason, it was important to him that she see him as more.

Of course, he had spent the night. Regina pressed her thighs tightly together as she thought about the way his wicked tongue had driven her crazy. Never had she imagined a man could take such delight in making a woman scream; never had she imagined she'd be able to have multiple orgasms, one right after another. He might not have kept her up all night this time, but he had definitely done the job. Though Regina had expected him to leave afterwards, Remy had spent the night, leaving only after making love in the shower one last time this morning. No, not "making love"—it was just sex. As enjoyable as last night and this morning had been, it was important that she called it what it was. There was no love involved here. She had to remember that.

And she was supposed to see him again tonight. Why she'd said yes, she still wasn't altogether sure. They had very little in common. Remy came from a highly influential family, both politically and financially. The

Chevaliers had been leaders in New Orleans for centuries. Regina came from a lower middle class family in New York City. While Remy was only close to his brother and cousins, Regina, being an only child, was extremely close to her parents. They meant the world to her. They would be highly disappointed in her if she were to get involved with someone like Remy. So why was she so drawn to him?

It had to be the sex. She had read about women who became addicted to a man. Though she couldn't really say she was addicted—not yet, anyway—she knew there was this animal magnetism that drew her to him. Remy oozed sexuality; he was a walking, talking promise of sin, from that wicked little grin to the way he moved. Of course she was attracted to him. He was so far outside her norm that he was bound to be irresistible on some level. She had two options: Ride out their fling until it ended, or put an end to it now. It would probably be wiser to put an end to it now.

"Dr. Booker? Your new patient, Mr. Smith, is on line three."

Mr. Smith was actually Remy, but she hadn't told her secretary that. Thanking the woman, she picked up the phone with a great deal more enthusiasm than she liked to admit.

"Hello?" Was it just her mind, or did she sound a little breathless?

"Hey, baby. Miss me?"

Regina smiled into the phone. Yes, but she wasn't about to admit it. "Hello Remy." *Stay cool, calm, and collected*, she told herself, feeling like a teenager with her first crush.

"Well? Do you miss me?"

The voice over the phone sent tiny quivers all through her body. What was it about a deep southern drawl anyway? It made her all needy and excited.

"Sure," she answered as nonchalantly as she could.

"Did you walk to work today?"

"Yes, why?"

"Meet me outside in five minutes."

She was outside in three, and Remy was waiting for her in a sporty little bluish-gray BMW M6 convertible. Despite spending the last eight hours talking herself out of seeing him again, Regina felt her heart take a little leap of joy just looking at him. She had to force herself to walk sedately to the door he held open for her. Dressed in simple jeans and a black t-shirt that hugged his lean muscles lovingly, he looked good enough to eat. His shiny black locks fell to the base of his neck in a perpetual windswept, boyish look. Though she couldn't see his eyes behind the mirrored sunglasses he wore, she knew they probably twinkled devilishly. He was a little devil.

"So, where are we going?" Regina asked as soon as Remy slid behind the wheel.

"It's a surprise," he winked at her, moving rapidly through traffic and onto the highway, headed east.

Regina melted into the butter-soft seat and watched the scenery. Though she had moved here at eighteen, for college, the raw beauty of Louisiana never failed to impress her. Majestic, moss-draped oak trees rose up to kiss the sky, while varieties of plants and flowers dressed the landscape in vivid, exotic colors. She noticed Remy was heading southeast on Delacroix Highway, and they were now just south of St. Bernard Parish. There were bayous on either side of the highway, lush with wildlife but not much else. After about thirty minutes, he pulled onto a narrow, red clay road lined with ancient trees. He had to slow the car to a crawl due to the huge ruts in the road. From the amount of dust that flew up around the vehicle, Regina guessed the road was seldom used. Intrigued, she sat up in her seat, still taking in the landscape.

"You know, most women would be concerned about a guy taking off to Timbuktu with nary a soul in sight," Remy laughed, seeing her increased excitement. "After all, who knows where you've gone or who you're with?"

Regina barely spared him a glance.

"Please," she dismissed the implication out of hand. "You are hardly a threat. You wouldn't have to rape anyone; you'd just charm their pants off. And it's not like you would harm a soul. Not physically, anyway. You don't have it in you."

"You sound mighty sure of that."

There was something in his voice: A self-mocking, remorseful quality generally found in the voice of someone who was guilty of serious infractions against others. It made her turn to study him carefully. Sure enough, there it was. His eyes were shadowed, a tick visible in his cheek, and his hands gripping the steering wheel so tightly his knuckles gleamed an almost unnatural pale white. Remy was suffering from extreme guilt. This kind of guilt didn't come from breaking someone's heart, or playing with an innocent's feelings. There was something considerably darker in his past he had yet to get over.

Not my problem, Regina told herself. *I cannot fix him. I will not attempt to fix him. I will enjoy the day and let it and him go.* It was her curse; she always attracted men who needed her far more as a therapist than as a girlfriend. Being the consummate therapist tended to mean she was undesirable as a girlfriend once a man got over whatever phobia or issue he was struggling with. Once they were over it, they were over her. It was getting old, and she was getting a little too old to be anyone's girlfriend.

Not that Remy was a viable candidate as a boyfriend, or anything deeper. Remy was fun, period. Fun that would soon be over.

"Remy, you never answered my question back in the office," Regina said suddenly. "How long was your longest relationship?"

She didn't think he would answer; his hands gripped the steering wheel so hard, she thought he might break the thing off completely. After a few minutes of silence, he sighed, his body slumping as if he were facing some sort of defeat.

"One year."

She instantly regretted the question. Whatever had happened between Remy and the unnamed girl had not been good. His voice had been gruff, and despite his relaxed posture, his jaw had been clenched. The terse reply made it clear he didn't want to talk about it. Still, the therapist inside her would not let it go.

"Would you care to expound?" she asked in a pleasant, cheery voice.

Remy glanced over at the woman in the passenger seat. He wasn't fooled by the non-threatening façade she put on. She had caught the anxiety behind his answer. Generally, when anyone asked him a question like that, his answer would be flip and light. He didn't believe for a second he had answered her because of her skills as a psychiatrist. He wanted her to know; he needed her to hear the whole, ugly story. Maybe if she could forgive him...

"Her name was Cherry Robichaud," he continued. "She was the cutest little redhead I had ever seen. Eyes like melted chocolate. I fell hard from the first minute I saw her. I was a senior in high school; she was a dropout working at a diner we all used to hang out at. She was from the bayou, completely unacceptable to my—to Lady Rienne."

He stopped, as if lost in the memories. Regina felt a sick churning in her stomach. He had loved her, this Cherry. He had obviously never been able to let it go. It shouldn't bother her this much, but it did. It hurt. Despite telling herself over and over again that this, whatever they were doing, was just for fun, Regina really *liked* Remy. Who wouldn't? He was absolutely gorgeous, funny, and the man could *cook*. She could never bring him home to her parents, but she didn't want to let him go either. She knew on an intellectual level it was not up to her; sooner or later, he would be gone. It didn't stop the wishing that lay just underneath her subconscious.

His voice shocked her out of her silent ruminations.

"She was a true wild child, while I was just playing at being one. She had me sneaking out, blowing off school. I even stole a car from some drunk old fisherman because she dared me to."

He grinned ruefully at the memory, and Regina found herself unjustifiably jealous of a ghost of the past. Now she really, *really* regretted the question.

"But of course Lady Rienne found out. She threatened me, threatened Cherry, threatened Cherry's family, but I couldn't let it go. The more interference from my dear grandmother, the more determined I became to be with her."

Regina winced at the sneer in which he said "*dear grandmother*." Yeah, Lady Rienne definitely deserved the animosity; especially after what the old woman tried to pull with Thierry and Angelique. But what Regina was hearing now was far deeper than animosity. There was a bone-deep hatred that sent chills down her back. This story was not going to end well.

As much as she didn't want hear the answer, she had to ask. "What happened?"

"Cherry got pregnant."

Regina wanted to throw up. Remy had a child out there somewhere? A child he never saw? No. No matter what Remy's issues were, he would not be the type to let his child grow up without being a part of his or her life. Regina didn't believe for a second that the consummate party boy he pretended to be was the real Remy. For one thing, he was actively seeking to spend time with her.

Regina didn't think he was hanging out with her for any reason other than to resolve whatever had happened to hurt him so bad. Like his cousin Thierry, he was too much the macho man to seek professional help. Like almost every other man in her life, he chose her because of her profession and dressed it up as "dating." Her head begin to pound as her stomach dropped; she had to end this today. It had never really bothered her before, but she was starting to feel the way she had no business feeling. She didn't want to hear anymore about Cherry Whatever-Her-Name-Was. She hated Cherry. At least the "cute little redhead" had what Regina would never have—the true affection of Remy Chevalier. Damn, that hurt.

"She thought I was going to marry her," Remy continued, completely unaware of Regina's distress. "I liked her. God knows, I thought she was one hot little... Well, I liked her anyway."

Wait, *liked*? Didn't he love her? She felt like a complete bitch, but Regina was beginning to feel a hell of a lot better. It was awful, she knew, but she couldn't help but take solace in his words.

"But like I said, Cherry was wild," he went on. "We did things together I had only seen in porn. Which is why I couldn't be sure..."

"Wait," Regina cut him off, sitting up in avid interest now. "What do you mean you couldn't be sure?"

Remy actually started to blush. "We, uh, sometimes weren't alone."

"And you let her? With other men?"

Nope, Regina thought, *he didn't love her*. From what she had seen, men who shared the women they loved were rare. Rarely was a threesome a true *ménage*, with all three sharing an equal amount of love and admiration with one another. Sometimes it was bisexual, sometimes not, but always with a great deal of affection going three ways. Remy's had definitely not been one of those rare cases. Not as a senior in high school. That had been sexual exploration.

"Cherry was more like my best friend than a girlfriend," he clarified. "If I loved her at all, it was more like the way I love Thierry, Aubrey or Piers."

Regina took note he didn't mention his twin, Rance. Interesting.

"But you did sleep with her," Regina reminded him. "So it couldn't have been exactly like you feel for your cousins."

"I guess not," he conceded. "But it was close. Near the end, we didn't have sex at all. That was another reason I doubted the baby could be mine. She would have known sooner."

"So what happened?" She had to know.

"I told her I wouldn't marry her, that I couldn't marry her because I didn't love her like that. As a direct result, she died."

Of all the things Regina had imagined, that wasn't one of them. It was far, far worse. Now she understood why Remy shied away from serious relationships. He blamed himself for Cherry's death. Not because he couldn't marry her and give a name to her unborn child who might or might not have been his. But because he didn't love her. The idiot blamed himself for not loving a woman who may or may not have loved him back.

"You blame yourself, don't you?" She hadn't meant for it to sound like an accusation, but it did.

"Oh, I don't blame myself for not loving her," Remy contradicted Regina's silent analysis. "I blame myself for bring my criminal grandmother into her life. Cherry went to Lady Rienne, hoping the old lady would either make me marry her, or at least provide for her. Of course, the old woman did neither. She threatened Cherry again, this time with prison for trying to extort money. When Cherry didn't believe her, she called a sheriff she had in her pocket and had Cherry locked up for the night. They couldn't hold her. There was nothing to charge her with, but Cherry didn't know that. She hung herself in the cell, thinking her life was over."

CHAPTER FIVE

There was absolute silence in the car for the rest of the drive. Remy played the ugly scene over and over in his mind. He had been furious with his grandmother, but in the end, there was nothing he could do. Cherry was dead and nothing could bring her back. Lady Rienne hadn't even had the soul to be remorseful. She had just shrugged it off, saying simply, "Good riddance to swamp trash."

It was that incident that had spurred Remy to find a way out from under her thumb. He had dug and dug and dug until he finally found something to hold over the evil witch's head. It had taken years, but he knew it would be there. One did not become the most powerful matriarch in Louisiana without having skeletons, and as it turned out, Lady Rienne's could fill a mansion's worth of closets.

As hard as reliving the past had been, he felt better having said it all out loud. His brother and cousins only knew part of the story; Regina was the only person to whom he had told the whole sordid tale. He had no idea why he'd told her. Sure, she was damn good at what she did, but he knew it wasn't her professional training that had him singing like a bird. Even if that was part of it, it wasn't her skills as a therapist that drove him to bring her out here to his secret little hideaway. Three days ago, he'd thought all he wanted from Regina was to see her with her hair down. As soon as he'd touched her, tasted her, he couldn't seem to get enough. Now he woke up wanting to feel her; his mouth felt bereft without her taste on his lips. Had it really only been three days?

Regina stared out of the car window, a growing sense of trepidation coming over her. She had imagined many different scenarios to explain why Remy was afraid to commit to one person. Now she knew; he wasn't so much afraid to commit as he was disinclined to commit. Seriously disinclined. He had suffered from his inability to love a woman he thought needed him, and he felt a great deal of guilt. Now that it was out in the open, a part of that guilt would inevitably be relieved, which meant he was on the road to recovery. Not that it would be easy to let go of something he had held onto for so long, but eventually he would let go. He didn't really need Regina anymore, and it had only taken three lousy days. That had to be some kind of record, even for her.

No point in crying over spilt milk, she told herself. She would just enjoy the rest of the afternoon, and maybe that night. But this definitely had to be the last time. No more putting it off. And no more allowing men who needed therapy through her door. This was getting old. Or maybe Remy had taken more from her in the very short time they'd had together. Who knew attachment could grow in such a short time?

You did, she admitted to herself. It wasn't uncommon at all. While Thierry had loved his wife for years, Angelique had fallen for Thierry, hard, in a shockingly short amount of time. Life was littered with tales of love, or at least serious lust, at first sight. Too bad it was completely one-sided in this case. Remy might not understand what he was feeling or what he was after, but she did. It was her job to know such things. It didn't stop the sharp pain in her chest that made it difficult to breathe.

She stared un-seeing at the scenery outside the window. She also failed to notice that the car had come to a complete stop.

"We're here," Remy told her, watching her carefully.

Something was wrong. Because she had been so quiet since his revelation, he couldn't help but worry. What if she thought him to be the heartless jackass he believed himself to be for so long? It was Regina who'd given him courage to revisit the whole thing in his head over the last couple of days. Every second he was away from her, he went over different scenarios in his head again and again. None of them had ended well. It had been a doomed situation from the moment Cherry had announced her pregnancy.

No matter what, it would have ended badly. Cherry wasn't capable of being with one man—not to judge her, but it was just the way she was. He was not capable of accepting that kind of relationship, especially not if he had married her. Eventually, they would have ended up hating each other had he offered her marriage. He had promised to support Cherry no matter what, financially as well as emotionally, but that hadn't been enough. Cherry had wanted the ring and the security she thought would come with the Chevalier name. Little did she know, he had done her a favor by denying her that name and all that came with it. Regina was smart enough to figure all that out by herself, knowing his family as she did. So why the silent treatment? Was it the admission of his wild sexual past? Maybe she was turned off by everything—his family, the situation with Cherry, his grandmother.

Jumping out of the car, Remy quickly made his way around to open the door for her. He didn't want to miss a second of her reaction to the place.

"Oh my God!"

Before her stood a huge antebellum mansion. Having lived in Louisiana since her freshman year at college, Regina had seen a southern mansion or two, but this one was the most beautiful place she had seen by far. Whitewashed columns framed the entire house, which had to be bigger than the entire block she lived on. The second floor had a wrap-around balcony, with French doors in the front. Every room on the second floor probably had access to the balcony. Magnolia trees in full bloom surrounded the house. From what she could see, someone was lovingly restoring the grand old place to its original splendor.

Although it was definitely a plantation house, the telltale signs of a former plantation were absent. The house was located directly in the middle of an elevated meadow. All around the outer yard was pure wild Louisiana. It was as if someone had built this house in the middle of nowhere.

"Is this place yours?" Regina asked in wonder. Who would have thought Remy would be in possession of a place like this?

"Yep," he answered proudly. "All mine."

"Was it a plantation?" she had to know. It would be a shame if it was. How could a place so beautiful have once been a testament to one of the darkest times in American history?

"Actually, it wasn't. One of my ancestors built it for his wife. She refused to own slaves, so all their servants were paid. Come on, let me show you around."

There was quite a bit more to the story, but he wanted to save the rest until later. For now, he needed to show her what he hoped would one day be his home. He was unsure why it was important he had her approval, but it was. He wanted her to love the house every bit as much as he did. He took her into the half-finished kitchen, explaining all the updates he had specified and how he envisioned the finished project. It was his favorite room in the house; he wanted everything to be just right. From there he took her around the rest of the downstairs floor, through the dining room to the formal parlor, the massive study, then to the slightly smaller library.

"This would be a great place for a home office," Regina mused, looking around the airy room.

The off-handed comment warmed Remy to his bones. Yes, it would make a great home office; a place she could see patients if she chose, or work on studies or papers. It occurred to him in that moment that the reason it was so important for her to love this place was that he wanted her here with him. No one, not even his brother, knew about this house. It had always been his little secret.

Leaning against the walls, he watched as she roamed the space as if she were mentally painting the walls and filling the room with furniture. He liked her; *really* liked her. He fell in and out of lust on a regular basis, but he had never honestly *liked* a woman before; at least, not the way he felt about Regina Belle at this very moment. He may have had a few women he considered friends; well, one actually. Thierry's wife Angelique was really the only woman he had allowed to get close. Angelique was also one of Regina's best friends. While Remy loved Angel like a sister, what he felt for her couldn't come close to what he was beginning to feel for Regina.

It was crazy—they had only known each other for a short time, had only began to sleep together in the last few days, but Remy couldn't deny what was right in front of his

face. He was falling in love with her. Hard. He could feel
Regina pulling away from the magnetic attraction they had,
and it drove him crazy. He couldn't allow her to retreat
from him; he wouldn't let her turn her back on what could
be. He had no idea where this would lead, but he damned
sure wanted to find out.

"Let me show you the rest of the house," Remy
said, taking her hand.

*****

Regina let the magic of the mansion wash over her
as Remy led her from room to room. It was impossible not
to get caught up in Remy's excitement. She found herself
seeing what he saw, all that the place could be one day.
They spent the rest of the afternoon exploring room after
room, discussing what should be done in each. He
encouraged her input, listening carefully to all her
suggestions. After they had gone through every room,
Remy surprised her with a gourmet meal from a basket she
hadn't noticed in the backseat. They sat on the veranda,
watching the sunset bathe the surrounding vegetation in the
reddish purple of twilight. Regina was sorry when they
packed up to go. It was for the best, though. For a little
while, she had imagined herself living here with Remy.
That would never happen, could never happen. Remy was
not for her.

Masking her melancholy thoughts, she was able to
appear chipper on the ride back to the city. She noticed
Remy drove a great deal slower on the drive back. She
didn't mind. The extra time helped her get a hold on her
jumbled feelings. She liked Remy. The realization

surprised her. She had always considered him incredibly sexy and more than a little funny. She was pleasantly surprised to find that there was so much more underneath his wisecracking veneer. He was a great guy and would make a hell of a husband for some woman. It hurt more than a little that she wouldn't be that woman.

When Remy pulled up in front of her small house, Regina planned on ending it then and there... until Remy turned those aqua eyes at her. There was no teasing, no jokes or sarcastic remarks.

"Regina Belle, I don't want today to end."

His voice was deeper than usual, gruff with desire. Regina shivered when he reached out to caress her face. How could she possibly say no? Her lips parted willingly as he leaned down to gave her the softest, sweetest kiss she had ever experienced in her life.

"Let me spend the night with you, Regina," he whispered against her lips. "Please don't send me away."

How could she say no to that?

His kisses were sweet and slow, drugging her senses and melting her from the inside out. He undressed her with deliberate slowness; each inch of exposed skin was baptized with a caress of his lips. By the time she was finally free of her restrictive clothing, she was burning with need.

"Please, Remy," Regina pleaded. "I need you." Just one more time, just for tonight, she wanted to pretend she could keep him, that he was all hers.

Despite her pleading, Remy took his time. He knew she was planning on taking a step back from him. He couldn't let her do it. Instead of teasing or being his usual sardonic self, he decided to let her see exactly what he felt.

47

When he asked to stay the night, he had been afraid. He was afraid she'd say no, even more afraid she'd say yes. Everything about Regina scared the shit out of him. Even now, with her laying on the bed begging for his touch, he was terrified by all the feelings she inspired in him. She was so beautiful, so intelligent. Remy wished like hell he could know why she was so reluctant to take him seriously.

So he decided to show her all that he felt. He ran his hands over her baby-soft skin, loving the way she squirmed when he trailed his tongue from her neck to her belly button. He was so hard he could drive nails, but he was determined to hold off. He wanted to make love to her slowly, until they were both out of their minds with desire. Moving down her body, he stopped to place little love bites on her lower abdomen and her inner thigh, until he was seated right in front of her glistening pussy. Closing his eyes, Remy inhaled deeply. Delicious. He wanted so much to dive in, to drive her to the edge over and over again. Reigning in his impulses, he went slowly; licking and gently suckling, he alternated between her labia and her clit. Her cries drove him crazy; it was all he could do not to let himself go completely. He kept his assault gentle, even when her body rocked in orgasm, her thighs clasping around his head as her hands gripped his hair.

"Please, Remy, I need you!"

Her call was music to his ears. He slid up her body, letting the light dusting of hair on his chest rub against her smooth skin. She trembled underneath him, her thighs spreading to accommodate him. She was so beautifully responsive, so in tune with his body. It was a wonder to him how he'd ever lived his life without her.

Regina arched her body, trying desperately to bring Remy where she needed him. He was driving her mad! No matter how much he touched her, it was not enough. She had never begged a man before, but she felt no shame in begging him now. She had never wanted or needed a man as much as she did Remy.

Finally, she felt his thickness probing her outer lips. She widened her hips, arching again, trying to bring him inside her. She almost cried when he retreated, not much, just enough to resist her prodding.

"Remy!" Regina cried out in frustration.

"Look at me, Regina," Remy commanded through clenched teeth.

Her eyes snapped to his without thought. She gasped as he slid inside her, inch by glorious inch, but she did not take her eyes off of his. His gaze held her captive as he began to move, stoking the fire to burn higher and brighter. She wished she could turn away from the truth burning brightly in his stare: He cared. It wasn't about sex or fun; he really cared for her. It shook her to her soul, sending her crashing over the edge with the force of a tidal wave. She screamed as her legs wrapped around his waist to pull him closer. He was hanging on by a thread; she knew that. Even though his eyes never left hers, she could feel the tension coursing throughout his body. She was determined to make *him* lose control. He had made love to her gently, as if she was the most precious thing in the world. Now she wanted him wild with lust. This would be their last night together—it had to be, for her own sanity. She wanted it to be everything.

Remy felt Regina's inner walls pulsate, squeezing his cock. She was unbearably tight and so damn good. He had wanted to make love to her gently, but when he felt her legs lock around him, he lost control. Gripping her hips, he slammed into her over and over again, turning her low moans into full-blown screams of pleasure.

"Oh, baby, you feel so damn good," he groaned into her neck, unable to hold back.

Regina met him thrust for thrust, clawing wildly at his back to bring him closer. Her feet pressed into his bucking buttocks, determined to urge him deeper, harder. She lost count of how many times he drove her over the edge until she felt him shaking. He surged forward one last time and as she screamed her release, he shouted his. It was so good she had tears in her eyes. How was she supposed to let him go? How could she possibly keep him?

CHAPTER SIX

Regina woke to the sound of determined pounding. What the heck was that? She tried to ignore it, snuggling deeper into Remy's side, but the noise persisted. She became vaguely aware that someone was pounding on her front door persistently. Whoever it was apparently refused to believe either someone was not home, or just didn't want to be bothered.

"Do you want me to get that?" Remy asked without moving.

Regina allowed herself a moment to feel his warmth surrounding her. How could just sleeping next to a man feel so damn good?

"No," she answered finally. "I'll get it."

She wanted to cry when Remy unwrapped his arm from around her waist and shifted his leg, which had been sandwiched between her own. Her body seemed to scream in protest as she rolled off the bed and shrugged into her robe. Stomping to the door, she went over what she would say to get whoever was out there to leave so she could crawl back in bed. What kind of person would bang this damn relentlessly at eight o'clock on a Saturday morning?

"Hurry back," Remy mumbled, burying his head in her pillow and inhaling deeply.

It was such a sweet gesture that Regina had to smile. Not for the first time, she wondered if he had any idea how he made a woman feel: Like she was the center of the universe. Such a little thing, like wanting to keep her scent surrounding him, made her feel so special.

Yeah, but how many other women in New Orleans felt just as "special" before Remy broke their hearts? the sensible side of her demanded. They had known each other for less than a month; they had been intimate less than a week. This was a fling, something to help Remy get over his insecurities so he could get on with his life. As long as she kept telling herself that, it would make letting him go easier. And no matter what, she had to let him go.

Dragging herself to the door, she forcibly turned her thoughts from Remy. There was no point in dwelling on him. Aggravated by the direction her mind was wandering, she pulled the door open with a fierce scowl marking her brow.

"Do you have any idea...?"

Regina's voice trailed off as she saw her parents standing, suitcase in hand, at her doorstep. *Shit!* Horrified, she stood there blankly, feeling like a teenager caught with a boy in her room. What the hell was she going to do? How was she supposed to get Remy out of the house without her parents seeing him? What the hell were they doing here anyway?

"Well, that was certainly some welcome." Her mother, Marilyn Booker, pushed past her stunned daughter.

Regina shook herself out of her stupor and moved back to allow her parents into the house. *Shit!* She had to get Remy out of the house without them seeing him.

"What are you guys doing here?" Regina stammered. "I mean, I'm happy to see you. I'm just surprised."

"Your father has retired," Marilyn informed her flustered daughter. "We decided that instead of settling in Mississippi, as we originally planned, to come here to be close to our only child."

Regina turned her shocked eyes toward her father. He didn't say a word, just followed his wife into the house. Regina knew immediately that this had not been his idea. Her mother had been after Regina for the last couple of years, pushing her to settle down and start a family now that she was out of school and her practice was up and running. No doubt she had come with every intention of finally seeing that happen. Her father was just along for the ride.

"I'm sorry, Ma," Regina said hurriedly. "I know you've had a long drive. You drove down, right?"

"Of course we drove, child," her father groused. "Like I would let anybody else drive my car. I guess you sleeping the day away means you don't have breakfast ready either. Your mother wouldn't stop anywhere once we got across the state line."

Oh, thank God! Regina thought, then immediately felt like crap for thinking it. Still, it would give her a chance to get them, and then Remy, out of the house.

"I'm sorry, Pops," she smiled weakly. "I wasn't expecting company. I haven't gone grocery shopping in a good little while."

"That's why you're so skinny!" her mother declared. "Well, that's about to change. Come on, Reggie. I saw a diner just down the street. We can walk while Regina gets a room ready for us."

With that, Marilyn swung out of the front door she had just entered, always the perpetual ball of motion.

Reginald Booker followed more slowly in his wife's wake, muttering under his breath the entire time.

"Don't know why the woman would expect a person to cook breakfast for people she don't know are coming. Could've stopped at the diner before and saved some trouble."

While she agreed with his sentiment, Regina was damn glad they hadn't stopped to eat first. There was no telling what Remy would do just because he thought it would be funny.

She waited until she saw her parents disappear down the street before running back to the bedroom.

"Remy, I'm sorry, but you have to go."

Regina scurried around the room trying to locate all of his discarded clothes, throwing them over her shoulder in the general direction of the bed. Detecting no movement from Remy, she whirled around, making subconscious shooing motions with her hands.

"Did you hear me? You can't be here when my parents get back!"

Remy cocked his head, staring at her intently. Something in his cyan gaze sent warning bells clamoring off in her head. Whatever he was thinking was not going to be funny to her. Anger rushed through her at the possibilities. Did he think he could just play games with her life? Was he honestly thinking of saying something to her parents about the real reason he was here? Dear God, if he told her father they had slept together....

"I'm going to meet them eventually anyway, Regina. Why not now?"

Regina's imaginary rant skidded to a halt at his soft-spoken words. There hadn't been a hint of mockery or laughter in his voice. He seemed so—sincere.

"Because they will know why you're here."

Her response was every bit as measured as his words, though she felt far from cool, calm or collected.

Remy was constantly throwing her for a loop. And what did he mean he would meet her parents eventually?

"Regina, what do you think we've been doing?"

"I—I don't know what you mean."

She really didn't have time for this. Who knew how long her parents were going to be gone? And he wasn't even trying to put on his clothes!

"Remy, please."

She hated pleading, but she had to get him out of her house. There was no way she could explain away the presence of a naked white man in her bedroom. She may be an adult, but she didn't want to hurt or disrespect her parents, especially her father. She wanted to weep with relief as Remy finally stood and began to drag on his jeans, then his shirt. She was still wringing her hands together when he finished putting on his socks and shiny black boots and stood.

Despite her anxiousness to see him leave, she had to admit he was one fine-looking man as he stretched to his full height. He had left his shirt unbuttoned, showing the well-defined muscles of his chest, lightly sprinkled with jet-black hair. His jeans rode low on his narrow hips, allowing her eyes to follow the light line of hair that ran from the base of his navel down to where it disappeared into his pants. She was watching so intently, she didn't realize he was moving closer and closer, until her hand met with a wall of warm, hard flesh.

Regina blinked up at him at the contact. When had she reached her hand out? She couldn't remember. She began to pull her hand away, but he reached out to grab it, placing it back on his chest.

"Let me ask you something." His husky voice sent a bolt of reawakened need right through her. "What do you think we've been doing the last couple of days?"

"Having fun?" she offered with shrug.

She didn't know what Remy thought *he* was doing, but *she* had been falling hard for a man she could never have. It would be good to end this now, before things got too deep for her.

"As glad as I am to hear that, *cher*, I think we both know there's something more here. I want there to be something more, anyway."

Oh, God, it hurt to breathe! She closed her eyes against the pain. How could she possibly care for someone she had just met? How could there be all these damn *feelings* when they barely knew each other? She was a head shrink, a damn good one, and she knew all about projection—about feeling lost and alone, especially if someone close to you got married or had a child. She also knew what she was feeling right now, and it was none of those things. Whatever the heat between her and Remy was, it wasn't something you could study or diagnose. But it wasn't something they could allow to continue either.

"Remy, I won't lie to you and tell you I'm not attracted to you."

"Good."

"But there can be nothing more for us. Not with one another."

He didn't respond, which worried her immediately. He just kept that same damn steady gaze, like he was waiting for her to figure something out.

"I'm serious, Remy. This is not a relationship. It's not going to lead to one."

He stared a few moments longer, then bent down and touched his lips to hers. A soft whisper of a kiss, barely there at all. Then he turned to go.

"I'll be seeing you, Regina Belle," he threw over his shoulder.

It didn't sound like a goodbye. It sounded like a promise.

Regina shivered as she watched him leave. Her body already mourned the loss of his hard flesh pressed against her. More than that, she felt a strange sense of loss in her heart. How could making love a couple of times, okay a lot of times, make her heart cry out for someone like this? In the same moment, she told herself silently, *Shit! Sex, had sex*. It wasn't love, so they couldn't have been making love, right?

CHAPTER SEVEN

Regina met her best friends for Sunday brunch for the first time since her parents had arrived. They used to meet every Sunday, but since Angelique Dubois had become Mrs. Thierry Chevalier, the wife of one of the richest, most powerful men in the state, the Sunday brunches had gone by the wayside. It had only been two months since the drama that was Angelique and Thierry's wedding and reception. Four weeks since the last time Regina had last seen Remy.

"Why are you in such a hurry to find your parents a house?"

Regina turned her attention to the friend who had asked the question. Angelique looked radiant, happy. They had all worried that Angelique, the one with the least experience with men, would wind up married to whomever her mother chose for her. It had been a close call when she had become engaged to Paul Guidry, a snake of man if ever there was one. There was a time when Angel was probably the least happy of the group—until she met Thierry. Well, the unhappiest except for her cousin Solange, whom no one had seen since the infamous reception, and whom no one particularly missed. Solange had made her cousin's life a living hell, and to top it off, she had been spying on her for Angelique's mother. The night Thierry had shown off his African-American bride to the crème de la crème of New Orleans high society, Solange had dropped out of sight.

Thinking of that night made Regina's face burn in mortification. How could she have let Remy go down on her in a room full of people—*and liked it*?

"I would love it if I could live with my parents." Jade, sharp-as-a-tack lawyer, the eternal optimist and all-around sweetheart of the group, sighed.

"Does your mother constantly nag you for grandchildren and bemoan your lack of suitors?" Regina snapped. "Who the hell even uses that word anymore? *Suitors*?"

"Apparently, your mother," mumbled Katrina, Jade's law partner and proprietor of some of the most notorious strip and sex clubs in the greater New Orleans area.

"Seriously, Angel, doesn't your foundation have some home in a decent area I can buy?" Regina ignored Katrina. That woman had become grumpier and grumpier lately.

"Sorry," Angelique told her, shaking her head. "The homes the foundation buys and restores are for people who lost everything in the Hurricane."

Out of respect for Katrina, it was an unwritten rule never to say the name of the Hurricane. She decried it as insulting.

"Actually, the older couple down the street from me have decided to move to Florida," Jade offered. "They wanted me to help them sell their house. It's a good neighborhood, and the price probably won't be that much, considering."

She felt like kissing Jade for finally remembering she knew someone who was selling a house; finally, after Regina had been complaining about the damn price speculations for fifteen minutes. She had to get her parents out of her house. It had only been four weeks, but Regina was climbing the walls. Remy called daily, but there was no way in hell she could see him with two pairs of eyes watching her every move. Her mother had begun to go so far as to start talking to men in the grocery stores. Never mind that Regina couldn't seem to stand the thought of anyone being in her life, much less her bed—except for Remy.

Man, this was going to have to stop. Sure, he had called, but the few times Regina had actually answered the calls, she had managed to fob him off with one excuse or another. Sooner or later, he would stop calling. She didn't know what she would do then.

"I'll set up a time you can come over and look at their place," Jade was saying. "I know they want to move as soon as possible."

"Thanks, Jade," Regina sighed. "I don't know how much more of my mother's match-making I can take."

"Is that the only thing that's bothering you?" Angelique asked, eyeing her girlfriend shrewdly.

"What do you mean?" Regina looked everywhere but at Angelique.

"Remy's been over a lot lately," Angelique replied, absently stirring her sweet tea while her eyes stayed on Regina. "He seems awfully interested in what you've been up to recently."

Regina shrugged but didn't comment. Inside, her heart took a little leap of joy. Remy was asking about her! Did that mean he really cared? Was he missing her as much as she missed him? Or maybe he just missed having someone to talk to, someone who wouldn't judge him or act like everything he said was a joke. Her mood deflated once more. Maybe he wanted to explore the painful confession he had revealed the day he took her out to the country. Maybe it was just a passing curiosity. Damn it! She had to stop doing this to herself.

"Damn Chevalier men!" Katrina fairly growled. "What do they think? Because Thierry married a black woman, they all should? Is it some kind of sick curiosity? Some wierd obsession?"

All eyes turned to Katrina, who was generally cool, calm, and collected in any situation. The one thing Katrina *never* did was let a man get under her skin. And what the heck did that have to do with the Chevalier cousins?

"Uh, Katrina?" Jade asked uncertainly. "What makes you think they all want to get with black women just because Remy asked about Regina?"

"Don't you see? It's all some kind of game to them!" Katrina exploded. "Maybe not to Thierry. Anyone can see he is completely head over heels for Angel, but what the fuck is up with the rest of them? I mean, Rance can't be in the same room with Jade without panting over her." Katrina gestured wildly in Jade's direction. Jade bent her head and forlornly pushed salad around her plate.

"I don't think you could be further from the truth about that one," Jade sighed.

Regina's eyebrows rose as she watched her normally spirited friend look crestfallen and utterly dejected. And when the hell had Jade started ordering salads?

"Not to mention that damnable Aubrey, sneaky bastard that he is!" Katrina continued as the three other women stared at her in shock. What was so sneaky about Aubrey? He was the epitome of the absent-minded professor if ever there was one. "And now Remy is sniffing after Regina? He probably knows that he and all his sick-ass cousins are in serious need of therapy. You know what?" Katrina stopped and looked around at the wide-eyed stares her little tirade had evoked. "Forget it, I gotta go."

Fishing out some cash, she haphazardly threw forty dollars on the table, more than her share of the meal, and stomped off.

"What the hell was that about?" Jade asked in awe as they watched Katrina stomp down the street.

"Hell if I know. But whatever it was, I think Aubrey had something to do with it," Regina offered.

"Aubrey?" Jade exclaimed. "He's so nice and quiet. He looks like the type Katrina would normally eat alive."

"Still waters run deep," Regina murmured, going over what Katrina had said.

She was probably right. Remy probably wanted some free therapy. In the end, didn't they all?

*****

Regina looked absently over her notes on her next patient. He wasn't due for another two hours, but she wanted to be prepared; plus she had the time. A manic-depressive transvestite with suicidal tendencies. It was the kind of case she would generally really enjoy, but all she saw when she looked down was a jumble of letters. For the first time in days, Remy hadn't called.

Had he met someone else? Had he met several somebodies? Had he just given up? In truth, she couldn't blame him, but it still hurt. What woman wouldn't want a man to follow her? She knew his not calling was probably for the best, but damn, she wanted to hear his voice. And she wanted to see his crooked smile, to smell his earthy scent. God, she missed the way his hands, slightly rough with innate strength, danced across her skin. His touch was electrifying and comforting at the same time. No one had ever set her nerve endings on fire the way he did. And those lips!

She groaned, sinking her head down on the desk. She was ruined for any other man. And after what, four mind-blowing experiences? How sad was that?

"Dr. Booker, can you take a last-minute appointment?" Regina's secretary broke through her morose thoughts. "He's here right now."

Sighing, Regina pulled herself together. She was a professional, damn it! She couldn't sit around pining for a man she couldn't have.

"Is it a new patient?" Regina asked. If so, she wanted to have a look at his referral before she agreed to take the case. She couldn't handle another self-obsessed rich boy with issues no one could help him with.

"No, it's a returning patient," the secretary responded, sounding far too pleased. Probably someone Regina had tried to refer to someone else. "It's—"

"I'll see him, send him in," Regina cut the woman off.

She was going to have to have a long talk with her flirty little secretary. A psychiatrist's office was no place to meet a man, but the young woman seemed bound and determined to do just that. Regina wasn't in the mood to hear which thirty-something captain of industry was barging in demanding an appointment. She'd get rid of whoever it was, then get back to work. Real work.

"Hello, Regina Belle."

Regina's head snapped up at the smooth, deep drawl. *Remy*. Her heart started racing erratically, despite her deep breathing. She drank in the sight as he sauntered into the office, closing the door quietly behind him and turning the lock. Sweet Lord, he was every bit as gorgeous as he'd been in her dreams. She had tried to convince herself that he didn't look that good in person, it was just her dreams manifesting a deep-seated want; a want she didn't need. She had told herself her mind was making him appear far more attractive than he really was. Now she knew that to be a lie.

His ebony locks looked carelessly windblown as always; his turquoise eyes sparkled. The beginnings of a five o'clock shadow graced his jaw, and despite the twinkle in his eyes, he looked tired.

"Hello, Remy," she answered, finding her voice. Damn, those jeans were definitely fitting him. The plain black t-shirt strained against his lean muscles. "What can I do for you?"

He's here to talk, she told herself. *He might have convinced himself he is here to see you, but he just needs someone to listen.*

She watched, barely breathing, as he moved closer, ignoring the chair in front of her desk to come right up to her, holding out his hand. Without thinking, she placed her hand in his, only to find her body hauled up out of her chair and into his arms. Without missing a beat, his lips claimed hers in fierce possession. She didn't even try to resist as he backed her against the desk, one large hand yanking up her skirt as he did so. His tongue stroked her own as his fingers dipped unerringly into her quickly flooding pussy. He was

64

relentless; two fingers lunged straight to her sweet spot while his thumb stroked her clit.

God, she missed this! He was able to play her body like a maestro played the violin. Her hands moved frantically to peel his t-shirt off his torso. She needed desperately to feel his hot skin against her own. It took several tugs before she could get the offending clothing out of the way. Remy didn't want to end his soul shattering kiss or remove his hands from her now dripping core. Her frenzied hands fumbled with the button fly of his jeans, seeking the cock she had dreamed about for weeks.

God, how she'd missed this! How she'd missed *him.*

"You thought I would just forget about this, *cher*?" Remy demanded roughly, pulling back to glare down at her.

Regina couldn't find her voice. His hand was still stroking deep inside her, robbing her of the ability to speak, or even to think clearly. He had that effect on her. Good intentions, promises to herself she would resist, flew right out the window whenever he touched her.

"This is my pussy; do you hear me, Regina Belle? Don't ever try to keep what is mine away from me again!"

She got wetter. He looked so fierce, those incredible blue-green eyes burning through her very soul. How could she not nod in agreement? What woman didn't want a man to want her with ferocious certainty?

"Say it, Regina Belle," Remy instructed. "Tell me you won't ever keep my pussy away from me again."

"I will never keep this pussy away from you again."

"*My* pussy, Regina. Tell me you will never keep *my* pussy away from me again."

Oh, God, she was going to come. Just a little bit more...

Remy stopped the probing of his fingers.

"I can't hear you, *cher*."

Damn, that deep Louisiana drawl was sexy.

"Your pussy, Remy," she rushed to assure him. "I will never keep your pussy away from you again."

"Damn straight!"

Instead of continuing his magnificent explorations, Remy pulled his fingers from her sopping cunt. She whimpered at the distressing loss, but couldn't tear her eyes away from the sight of him licking his hand clean. She didn't have long to feel bereft. Pulling her to the edge of the desk, Remy plunged inside her with one stroke. Regina sighed, closing her eyes and leaning back on her elbows.

"Look at me, Regina," he growled, holding himself completely still.

Regina's eyes snapped open. She had never seen Remy like this. Realization dawned gradually, shaking her perception of this beautiful man buried between her thighs. When he had been so forceful a few minutes ago, he hadn't done so to build sexual tension. Remy was deadly serious.

Once he was sure he had her complete attention, Remy began an unhurried, but fierce, pounding; drawing his heavy, steely cock out until only the head remained, only to slam it back into her. His leisurely-paced strokes knocked the breath from her body as his gaze held hers in an unbreakable grip.

"Two weeks," he growled, punctuating his words with a lunge from his hips. "Two fucking weeks. Do you know what I've been through? Do you know what you do to me?"

Regina didn't have an answer for him, not one that he would understand. There was no way she could introduce Remy to her parents, even if she wanted to. She had been so sure his interest in her would wane. He had unburdened his guilty conscience, hadn't he? It was all about his need to explore how the events from his past were affecting his present-day life, wasn't it? It wasn't about *her*. It couldn't be. Regina Belle Booker was not Remy's type. There was nothing glamorous or exciting about her.

"I can't fucking sleep without seeing your face, honey Belle. I can't stop thinking about you every minute of the day. You're underneath my skin, and I like you there. Don't ever think you can deny me what is mine."

His movements became faster as he spoke, his eyes never leaving her face. It was damn intoxicating; she was sprawled across her desk, her skirt around her waist, her blouse gaping open, her bra pushed underneath her breasts. Although his shirt was long gone, his jeans were merely pushed beneath his buttocks, where her feet now rested. She could see his abs flex every time he moved. Regina felt her climax building with the force of a category five hurricane, right there beneath the surface.

"And-you-are-MINE!"

She crashed over the edge, her body shuddering uncontrollably as he pumped all that he was into her. At that moment, she knew her heart and soul belonged to Remy Chevalier, and there wasn't a damn thing she could do about it.

CHAPTER EIGHT

Remy scrubbed his hands over his face. Two weeks. It had been two fucking weeks since he had last seen Regina, and she was still dodging him. He was certain after the whole episode in her office she would stop running from him, but if anything, it had only made her run harder and faster. Even though she wouldn't take his calls, he still found himself dialing her number every day, several times a day. What the hell was wrong with him? Why couldn't he get her out of his system? She obviously had every intention of turning her back on the attraction he knew she felt. Why did he care so damn much?

Even as he asked himself the question, he already knew. He had known a month ago. There was just something about the poised, reserved Regina Belle Booker that set his blood on fire. On some level, he guessed he'd known that before he had ever touched her. And once he'd touched her, he'd known he would never want to touch another woman again. Why would he? She was his perfect foil—calm where he was excitable, rational where he was emotional. That was the problem. Regina was trying to rationalize this... whatever it was they were going through. Instead of just going with the wild, instantaneous magnetism between them, she was busy explaining it away.

Maybe he shouldn't have told her about Cherry. He had carried a great deal of guilt over Cherry's death, but just talking with Regina about it had really helped him put everything in perspective. He had been carrying around the guilt of a child. Now, he was able to see the entire situation as a man. There was nothing he could have done, not after Cherry had gone to Lady Rienne. Had she really trusted him, she would have asked him for help. Instead, she had used his friendship as a way out, trying to blackmail and manipulate. Yeah, Cherry was young, and God knows she didn't deserve what had happened to her at the hands of his grandmother. But in the end, there was nothing he could have done to stop the tragedy that had occurred.

But then again, Remy was convinced that Regina was using his past with Cherry as a convenient excuse. Regina was running from more than the story he'd told her. She was an intelligent, insightful woman. After the last time he saw her, she knew damn well he wasn't into her to work out some tragedy in his past. He'd made that abundantly clear.

Remy cringed as he thought back to the way he had taken her. He'd had her sprawled across her desk, in the chair, and on the chaise she kept by the large bay windows. He had been a man possessed, needing desperately to brand her as his. But it hadn't been enough. Despite the guilt he felt in taking her so forcefully, he couldn't help getting hard as steel remembering the way she had felt wrapped around his dick. Every moan, every sigh, every scream had sounded like music to his ears. She'd been soft and yielding beneath him, spread out like a feast all for him. Beautiful.

Moaning softly, he rested his head against the steering wheel. Damn, he was wild about that woman. Every passing day without her seemed like a life sentence. He had to get her back. Not that he'd ever really had her in the first place. Now he was so desperate, he was about to do the one thing Remy Chevalier never did—ask for help.

"Remy, is there a reason you're sitting outside my house?"

*****

"He said what?!?"

Regina shrugged, picking at the blanket thrown across Katrina's soft, comforting brown leather couch. Looking around, she mentally shook her head. She couldn't have picked a worse place to go if she was looking for comfort. But then again, that wasn't what she was looking for. A cold dose of reality was what she needed, and she couldn't think of a better person to give it to her than Katrina.

"Look, Katrina, what I said or what he said during the... act, doesn't really matter."

"Doesn't it?" Katrina grinned, plopping down beside her. "Some say that what you say during an erotic high is almost the same thing as what you say when you're drunk. The highs are similar, but the overall effects are different." Pausing for effect, Katrina leaned forward and stared directly into Regina's eyes. "So, Ms. Psychiatrist, if what people say when they're drunk is nothing more than suppressed truth, whatever you said to Remy, and whatever he said to you, is truth, on some level."

"That's bullshit and you know it! How many men have told lie after lie just to get in your pants?"

"Yes, Regina, dear, but that's to get *into* the panties. Once a man is in, there's no longer a reason to lie."

Sometimes Regina hated Katrina as much as she loved her.

"It may be true in the heat of the moment," Regina countered. "But that doesn't mean a damn thing afterwards. As much as I might enjoy having *sex* with Remy, it doesn't mean I want a *relationship* with him."

"Uh huh."

Regina really didn't like the sound of that.

But then, what was the point in trying to convince Katrina when she couldn't even convince herself? She had been so sure Remy was merely working out his issues while having a little fun. But that was not the impression he'd made two weeks ago. She still got weak in the knees by just thinking about all the things he had done to her. She had trouble sitting at her desk and looking at the dark polished wood without getting wet. She couldn't bring herself to offer a patient her chaise, as had previously been her habit. Most of all, she had a hell of a time looking her secretary in the eye. There was no way in hell the woman hadn't heard them, and there was no mistaking exactly why Regina had cancelled all the rest of her appointments that day.

"Katrina, it wouldn't work out. We're too different. I doubt if Remy has ever taken anything seriously in his life."

That wasn't exactly true, but Katrina didn't need to know that. Regina was well aware that with the exception of their first encounter, Remy had been deadly serious. A little too serious for comfort. Even if her parents had not moved here, she wouldn't have taken the chance of seeing where their fling would lead. She couldn't risk falling in love with someone like Remy.

Too bad it was too late. She was in deep. Every day, it took everything she had in her not to call him, not to answer his calls.

"Why are you here, Regina?" Katrina cut into her morose thoughts.

"I thought I was here to talk to a friend," Regina snapped, deliberately ignoring the meaning behind Katrina's question. She knew what the other woman was really asking her. Why was she fighting her insane attraction to a single, sexy, heterosexual male?

"I'm sorry, sweetie, but if it's a fight your looking for, I am not the one to give it to you. Why won't you tell me the real reason you don't want to get involved with Remy?"

"He's white." Regina felt sour to her stomach just saying it. It sounded ugly; harsh and prejudiced, even to her own ears.

"Is that your own hang-up, or someone else's?"

Sometimes Katrina was far too intuitive.

"Does it matter?"

"Hell yeah, it matters!" Katrina exploded. "You can't live your life by someone else's rules, Regina. Very few people get the change at love, or intense lust, or whatever the hell you want to call it."

"You don't understand," Regina sighed, wanting to shout, scream, and run around pulling out her hair. "It would hurt my dad. Really hurt him. I can't do that, Katrina."

"Well," Katrina shrugged, shaking her head at her friend. "If that's the way you feel, be prepared to be dissatisfied with what you wind up with. Just keep in mind: While you're living your entire life for your parents, what are you going to end up having after they're gone? And when, exactly, can you start living for you?"

*****

"Regina? Dr. Regina Booker?" Thierry asked incredulously. "Wow, that's one I never saw coming."

"I don't know what to do," Remy groused, swigging down half the bottle of beer Thierry had handed him. "She keeps avoiding me. She won't answer my calls. I know I probably messed up by going to her office like that, but what the hell was I supposed to do? Let her just walk out of my life?"

For the first time in a very long time, Thierry was stumped. He could do little more than stare at Remy. Remy, the perennial playboy, the man who took nothing seriously, was in love. Not in lust, not merely captivated for the moment, but head over heels. He watched as his younger cousin paced the den, absently picking up a knick-knack here and there before replacing it. He wasn't moping; not exactly. There were no dramatic sighs, no "*Oh, woe is me*" comments. It seemed to Thierry that his cousin was just on a quest to understand the woman who perplexed him—and he had a cold, hard determination to capture said woman and make her his. It was a sentiment Thierry understood completely.

"Have you tried talking to her about it?"

It was lame advice, Thierry knew, but he was at a complete loss. He really didn't have these issues with Angelique. Not to this extent anyway. Angelique had been sweet and completely innocent. She had trusted him from the start. Regina was a bit more world-weary. In her profession, she had to be. She was used to dealing with the very worst of the human psyche.

"Have you ever tried talking to a psychiatrist who is convinced she has you all figured out?" Remy snapped. "At first she thought I was just seeing her to 'work out my

73

issues.'" He used finger-quotes to emphasize his disdain for that particular point of view. Thierry swallowed a laugh and tried to look properly empathetic. "Then, she claimed I was simply grateful for the supposed breakthrough or whatever. Now, she claims I'm just fascinated by you and Angel. She said I was trying to recreate what you two have in my own life, because I'm missing something!"

Remy threw himself down on the sofa with a snort of disgust after his little tirade.

"Is any of that true?" Thierry inquired, completely fascinated now.

Remy shot his cousin a look of pure disgust, but otherwise didn't respond. Thierry scratched his head, perplexed. Unlike Remy, he found each of the excuses Regina had given him completely plausible; that is, they would have been plausible if he didn't know Remy. Whatever issues he may have had from childhood, or young adulthood, would definitely not be a factor in whom Remy chose to love. As for Remy trying to capture what Thierry had with Angelique, that was a definite possibility; but what was so wrong with that? Didn't everyone want the same kind of love they read about or saw in the movies? It was one of the reasons romance books sold more than any other genre; it was why Hollywood pumped out romantic movies. Were women the only ones who longed for a deep, meaningful connection?

"Do you think she meant because she's black?" Thierry asked cautiously. As much as he hated to admit it, the thought did dance across his mind. Had Remy conflated love with an interracial relationship?

"Are you serious?" Remy stared at Thierry like he had suddenly grown horns. "You think I want Regina because she's *black*?"

Thierry shrugged and watched his cousin intently. If there was anything he was a master of, it was reading people. If that was one of the underlying reasons why Remy was so attracted to Regina, he would know.

"Fuck you, Thierry!" Remy surged to his feet and stomped to stand eye to eye with the one person he'd thought would actually help him. "I don't know why Regina got under my skin, but it damn sure wasn't her race! Do you think I want Lady Rienne breathing down my neck? As much as she chooses to ignore me now, do you really think she's going to take this one lying down? I may not be able to stand the old lady, but I'll be damned if I want to *invite* the old bat to interfering in my life again. Hell, it would be easier if I wanted to marry some trailer trash bimbo, than it will be if I marry Regina!"

"Are you sure you want to subject Regina to that?" Thierry didn't raise his voice as Remy had done. He had his answer. The poor boy was head over heels for the good doctor. She had better wrap her head around being Mrs. Regina Chevalier, because Remy wasn't going to have it any other way.

Remy suddenly looked so lost, Thierry almost wanted to hug him—almost. He generally couldn't stand that kind of affection from anyone but Angelique.

"I don't have a choice," Remy answered softly. "I will protect her with my life, but I just can't let her go."

CHAPTER NINE

Regina critically assessed her reflection. Why had she given in to her mother and agreed to a blind date? And when the hell had she started letting her mother fix her up? *When you decided you didn't want to see Remy anymore,* her snarky inner voice replied. She had found that she couldn't stand to talk to other men, couldn't stand to think of them as anything beyond friends. Lord knows she had tried. Remy hadn't called in over a week, and it had been three long weeks since she had seen him. Had he given up? A razor-sharp pang of fear ripped through her at the thought. Even though she had turned him away, she didn't want him to give up this easily.

If he cared, he would be camped out on my damn doorstep! It was a perverse notion, but Regina had long passed the point of being rational when it came to Remy. *He could have come back to my office. He could shower me with flowers. He could...*

Regina stopped her mental rant and looked into the mirror once more. God, *she* needed therapy. Maybe Katrina was right. Maybe she was giving up on something real because she was afraid of disappointing her parents. They had been so proud of her when she'd graduated from college, and twice as proud when she'd graduated medical school. They had given her everything she needed to succeed. She couldn't bear the thought of disappointing them, or worse, having them turn away from her. But then again, she didn't want to spend the rest of her life wondering what could have happened between her and Remy.

The doorbell cut off her ruminations. Wiping away the tear that had escaped from her eye despite her best efforts, she quickly checked her reflection once more, grabbed her purse, and made her way to the door. The sooner she left, the sooner she could come home and lick her wounds.

*****

I am not stalking her, I am just making sure she's all right, Remy told himself as he huddled behind the wheel of his car. Even as he thought it, he felt like a sick fool. He had sat outside her house every day for the past week. Though he had finally stopped calling her, calls which she never answered, he had to see her. He had to make sure she was... Who the hell was he trying to fool? He wanted to see if she had replaced him. He thought maybe if he saw her with someone else, he'd be able to move on. It was a bald-faced lie, but it made him feel better.

Feeling like the unbalanced idiot he had indeed become, he slumped his head on the steering wheel. He really did need therapy. Stalking a woman was not cool, and it was so not him. But Regina did that to him. She knocked him completely off balance. He had never in his life felt so turned inside out, not knowing whether to howl and curse the Fates or to cry. At least she hadn't been seeing anyone else. He wasn't too sure what he would do if he saw another man....

Just as he looked up, he saw what had to be a linebacker walk up to her front door. The man had to be six-foot-three at the very least, his own august height, wearing a tailored suit and driving a flashy Rolls Royce. His own flashy car aside, Remy hated him on sight. Flashy. Nouveau riche. All the blue blood in his veins rushed immediately to the fore, making him feel like a complete ass. But damn it to all hell and back, what was the man doing outside his woman's door? Sitting up, Remy counted the seconds until the door opened. If that man stepped one foot inside Regina's house, he was coming after him. He released a pent-up breath as Regina stepped outside, shaking the man's hand as if they had never met. Blind date—had to be, by the way she was keeping careful physical distance. And from the pleasant but distant smile on her face, Regina was not impressed. Especially when he showed her to the passenger side door and walked around the car to open his own. She gave a little frown before opening her own door and climbed into the car. Perfect.

A plan formed in his mind as he followed the flashy car out of her neighborhood, down into the more metropolitan downtown area. Whoever this guy was, he was definitely not a native, choosing one of those Yankee-type restaurants that had recently sprung up to cater to the sharks looking to take advantage of other's misfortunes after Hurricane Katrina. The place was more New York than New Orleans. Although Regina was herself a transplant, Remy instinctively knew she would hate it. Regina may be reserved, even a little uptight, but she was genuine. Having fed her on more than one occasion, Remy knew she preferred real food to any kind of overpriced snobby cuisine.

He watched the couple from across the street for a few moments before picking up his cell. If Regina Belle thought she was going to date her way into forgetting him, she was in for a rude awakening. *Well, maybe not so rude,* he thought with a smile, *but definitely enlightening.* He was tired of giving her space to figure out how she felt. He knew how he felt, and he was positive that everything that he was feeling, she was feeling too. Leave it to a therapist to overanalyze what was as natural as the sun rising in the morning.

Regina Belle was his woman. He was obviously going have to explain that to her real nice and slow, because apparently, she kept forgetting.

*****

Regina watched her date, Samuel Something-or-other, as he tried to covertly check out their waiter. The man might have thought he was on the down low, but he was painfully obvious to anyone willing to look hard enough. Oh, he said all the right things, made all the right moves, but his heart wasn't in it. It was like he had tried to memorize some dating manual. After the first twenty minutes, Regina carefully steered the subject away from the usual getting-to-know-you chitchat of a regular date and started to talk to Sammy-boy as if he were one of her girlfriends.

Worked like a charm. She doubted he even realized how he sounded as he gushed about *Dancing with the Stars* and *American Idol.* He talked knowledgably about clothing, shoes, and every starlet who'd burst on the scene for the last five years. It was stereotypical, she knew, but if all that didn't give him away, the way he twisted his wrists as he spoke was a dead giveaway.

She didn't have to wonder why he had agreed to go out with her. Her mother had probably told him she was in the market for a husband. Sammy was an up-and-coming attorney looking to translate his growing popularity as a lawyer into political office. He would need a wife. He probably thought Regina was desperate enough not to look too closely, thanks to her mother's attitude.

God, I hope and pray I never get that desperate. Regina mentally shook her head. *Sorry, Sammy, but I'm not your girl.*

Every so often, it seemed that Samuel remembered he was supposed to be on a date and halfheartedly tried to woo her. About halfway through the dinner, Regina had had enough. First of all, she could barely stomach the bad fusion cuisine that was supposed to incorporate Cajun and Southern food into lighter, healthier fare. There was no discernable seasoning, and everything tasted like it had been boiled in plain water. Secondly, if Sammy and the waiter's byplay got any hotter, they would soon be going at it right on the table.

"So, Sammy, how long have you known you're gay?" Regina asked in a conversational tone.

His fork stopped halfway to his mouth as he gaped at her. Feeling a little guilty for busting him out so abruptly, she reached over and took his other hand in her smaller one.

"I'm sorry, Samuel," she soothed. "I didn't mean to make you uncomfortable."

Putting his fork down, he looked at her with a mixture of fear and horror. Realizing he probably thought she was threatening him in some way, Regina rushed to reassure him.

"Your secret, if it is a secret, is safe with me. I just think it's a shame you can't openly be who you are."

He remained quiet for so long, she feared he was going to have some kind of break down or adverse reaction. Slowly removing her hand, she braced for the backlash. Men who are trying to hide their sexuality generally don't like to be outed, especially by the women they're trying to fool. She'd been stupid to allow her irritation at the situation to overrule her common sense.

"Was I that obvious?" he asked finally in a low, defeated manner.

Regina breathed a sigh of relief. He was closer to coming out than she expected. At least he had accepted how he really was. It was so much harder to break through when the person refused to admit they were different from whatever social expectation they were trying to live up to.

"For someone in my profession, yeah, it was kind of obvious. Plus it is kind of hard to miss the smoldering looks between you and the waiter. I felt like I was intruding."

"Sorry about that." At least he had the decency to blush.

It really was too bad. He was a handsome guy. Maybe a little too handsome. His deep mocha-colored skin was smooth and even, his heavy dark eyebrows appeared to be shaped, even his fingers were manicured and polished with a flesh-colored polish. Very metrosexual. Before she knew it, he was pouring out how he had tried to conform, but he was finding it increasingly difficult. He had thought dating and eventually marrying some unsuspecting woman would be best for his career and maybe ease some of his "urges." Regina found herself in therapist mode, ensuring him it was okay to be who he was and promising not to divulge his secret—especially to her mother, who lived on the same street as he did. After doing the best she could, she gave him the number of a therapist he could talk to on a regular basis. It just couldn't be her.

"I think it would be best if you just took me home now," Regina concluded. She'd had enough; she wanted to go home.

CHAPTER TEN

Remy watched Didier disable Regina's home security alarm, then effortlessly pick the complicated lock on her front door.

"There ya go." Didier stepped back to let Remy inside.

Remy considered Thierry's right-hand man for a minute, trying to form the questions swirling inside his head into the right words.

"What exactly do you do for Thierry?" he asked at last.

"This and that," Didier shrugged, sliding his glove-clad hands into the back pockets of his faded denim jeans.

Everything about Didier DeCapêt screamed danger. Anyone with an ounce of street smarts would cross the street if they saw him sauntering their way. His cold gray eyes missed nothing; Remy had no doubt that disabling a home security alarm and picking a lock was little more than child's play to him. There was definitely a story behind the mysterious man.

"And how long have you been working for my cousin?"

"I don't work for Thierry. I used to work for... Boden, but I have never worked for Thierry."

"Didn't you help out with the thing with Lady Rienne and Angelique?" Now Remy was confused. When Thierry began his relationship with his wife, he knew Lady Rienne, their bat-shit crazy grandmother, would be a problem. Didier had helped Thierry head off threats from her as well as from Angelique's stepmother. The man had been downright instrumental in getting the two safely married and shooting down Lady Rienne's devious plans.

"Yeah, I helped. That doesn't mean I work for him."

"I specifically remember Thierry saying that you were his 'information' man." Remy wasn't sure why he kept digging. There was something about Didier, something familiar yet elusive. It was bugging the hell out of him.

"Doesn't mean I work for him." Didier gave him a sad little smile before turning and casually strolling away.

Remy shook his head as he watched the man leave. That was one puzzle that could wait for later. Gathering his supplies, Remy entered the house, locking the door behind him. From what he had seen, he doubted Regina would be out very late.

*****

Regina had never been so relieved to see her own front door. Samuel was a nice guy, but she was sick to death of working out other people's problems. If she had known becoming a psychiatrist would mean that she had to give free therapy to all her dates, she would have chosen another field.

If only that were true. You love your job. She sighed as she leaned against the door. She did love her job. She loved helping people, she loved unraveling the subconscious and finding an answer, or at least a cause. But she hated the effect it had on her personal life. Guys who didn't want to be analyzed stayed away, and those with some kind of subliminal need came out in droves. *Except for Remy.*

Unlike what she had originally thought, Remy had no real need to be "fixed." He might have had mixed emotions about his past, and she suspected some issues with his twin, but she had stopped lying to herself sometime in the past month. He hadn't been calling her several times a day because he wanted free therapy. There was a real connection between them, a magnetic attraction that she was too weak to fight. There was only one reason she pushed him away. Her father.

Wiping away the tear that escaped from her eye, she straightened and turned to unlock the front door. No sense crying over spilt milk. Remy had stopped calling. She hadn't seen or heard from him, and probably wouldn't. She had lost her chance.

And for what? For your father? He has someone who loves him, someone to grow old with. What do you have?

She swallowed back the sorrow threatening to crush her with regret. She had made a decision. Her parents were important to her; she couldn't intentionally hurt them. In the end, it didn't matter how much Remy made her feel in ways she'd never dreamed possible. It didn't matter how his touch set her body on fire with pure unadulterated need, or how his voice sent shivers up her spine, or a simple look made her flood her panties. It didn't matter how, when she was in his arms, she felt safe, secure, desirable, and wanted. And maybe she would never find another man who made her feel all of those things at once, but she could certainly find someone who made her feel one or two. That would be enough; it had to be.

Just as she stepped through the door, it slammed behind her and an immense, firm body pressed her own smaller frame against the door. Though she was curious, she didn't panic. The increase of her heart rate or the heaviness of her breathing had nothing to do with fear. Her body knew who held her captive before her brain had a chance to assimilate what was going on. Remy.

Inhaling deeply, Regna let his earthy scent deep into her lungs. Oh, Lord, had anything ever smelled so good? The heat of his skin seeped into her very bones, warming her from the inside out. She felt her body melt as his large hands traced her spine.

"Where ya been, Regina Belle?" She almost purred at the sound of his deep, rough voice. She never ceased to get wet whenever she heard it. "And more importantly, who were you with?"

Regina gulped. She couldn't answer; besides, it sounded like he already knew.

"No answer for me, sweetheart?"

She gasped as she felt a cool breeze against her upper thighs. He pulled up the hem of her dress slowly, allowing the smooth material to brush lightly against her skin.

"I won't ask you again, Regina Belle. Who was he?"

"It was a blind date." It was a waste of emotion to hate how weak her voice sounded, how breathless. It was also senseless to deny him anything at this point. He would get it all out of her eventually; she had absolutely no willpower when it came to him. "My mother set me up, but he was—is—gay."

"Why is your mother setting you up on dates, *cher*?"

Regina shivered anew at the rough growl against her ear. Her lower body thrust back, and her rear brushed against his rigid member. A soft moan escaped her lips as she pushed back farther. Oh, how she'd missed him. She squeezed her thighs together, trying to ease the ache caused just by being close to him. A sharp slap against one cheek of her questing buttocks triggered a low groan.

"Answer me, Regina Belle." The stern voice was followed by another stinging slap, this time on the opposite cheek. "Why is your mother setting you up on dates?"

"I think... I think..." She couldn't think at all. Remy's hand was beneath her dress, rubbing away the sting his little spanking had produced. She moaned, moving against the hand, completely forgetting to answer his question.

"What do you think, baby? Tell me." Remy nipped her earlobe, making it difficult to concentrate.

Regina had planned on being as honest as she could without telling him why her mother was trying to set her up with every eligible bachelor she came across. But then his hand traveled from her behind to place light strokes against the drenched crotch of her thong....

"She wants grandkids," Regina blurted without realizing what she'd said. "She wants to see me happily married with kids while she's young enough to enjoy them."

*****

Remy didn't think it was possible for him to get any harder, but Regina's words turned his simple hard-on into granite. Mrs. Regina Chevalier. Oh, hell yeah, that sounded perfect. He had planned on taking it slow, making love to his Regina so slowly it drove her crazy, but visions of her big with child, his child, sent him over the edge.

Turning her to face him, he took her lips in a savage, possessing kiss, his tongue mimicking what his dick would be doing very soon. The way she opened to his kiss, the way her body responded to his touch, he knew with every fiber of his being this was the one. His woman, the woman made to complete him. The epiphany sent a jolt of awareness through his body. He had to be inside her, he had to become a part of her—right now!

The little dress came apart in his hands, followed closely by the little scrap of material she called underwear. The sound of ripping material seemed to come from far away. She didn't protest, yielding beautifully to his insistent mouth and hands. In a heartbeat, he had her pinned against the door, her legs wrapped around his waist, his fly opened and his desperate cock at the mouth of her sex. Then he stopped.

Looking intently into her eyes, he steeled himself for what he had to say.

"Regina, look at me."

He watched as her eyes begun to focus, waiting until he was sure she could clearly hear and understand what he was about to say.

"Remy, we can talk later," Regina moaned, wiggling around, trying to force him inside her.

"No, we can't." He was adamant. He had to say this now. "I want you to listen to me and understand I mean what I say."

"What?" She didn't stop squirming, but he was reasonably sure she was listening.

"You can't keep doing this, sugar. I can't take it."

Finally, she stopped moving. Her soulful brown eyes looked up, and he lost his heart all over again.

"Doing what?"

She sounded frightened. Hell, she *looked* frightened. Her hands fisted on his shirt-clad shoulders as if to keep him from going anywhere. As if he could. And that was the point.

"You can't keep shutting me out. You can't keep trying to push me away. I will not let you go, Regina Belle. I can't. I won't spend another night without you. That's a promise, *cher*."

"Remy, I—"

He could read the denial in her expression, and he was having none of it. In one swift stroke, he buried his cock to the hilt, swallowing her gasp in his kiss. Once he was completely encased in her intoxicating, moist warmth, he forced himself to stay completely still, while kissing ever inch of her bare skin his lips could reach.

"Remy!" she wailed, desperately trying to rock her hips for relief.

Damn, she was sweet! They fit so perfectly, her vaginal walls clasping every inch of him. It felt so damn good; like coming home after a long, lonely time away. He wanted nothing more than to take her hard and fast, exerting his claim on her; but he had a point to make.

Slowly easing his way out until only the very tip remained, he fisted his hand in her hair, forcing her to face him.

"Open your eyes," he commanded.

As soon as her eyes opened, he drove his cock deep into her once more. She whimpered, clawing into his shoulder.

"You will not walk away from me again, Regina Belle. Do you understand me?"

He waited for his words to penetrate the wave of desire engulfing her before slowly withdrawing once more. Instead of driving home, he went slowly, tormenting her to the point where it was damn near killing *him*. He kept the deliberate pace until she was babbling incoherently, trying frantically to move her hips faster while trying to force him deeper at the same time.

"Damn it, Remy! Please!"

Lord knows he wanted to give in, but then he would be right back where he'd started. He had to make it perfectly clear, the only way he knew how, that this was not a once-a-month kind of thing.

"I want to hear you say it, Regina. Say it, and I will give you what you need."

He wasn't about to tell her what to say. She knew.

"I promise not to walk away from you again." And she wouldn't. She was too tired of running. She was miserable without him, no matter how impossible being with him was. She needed Remy like she needed air.

"And?" Like a dog with a bone, he couldn't let it go.

"I won't deny you, us, this. I won't deny you, Remy."

Something broke free inside him. It was almost as if he had waited his entire life for this moment. Anchoring her with one hand, Remy plowed into his woman over and over again. Her cries just seemed to spur him on as he drove her over the brink time after time. He couldn't stop; he didn't want to stop. Only when her legs pressed down on his hips in a painful lock and her pussy convulsed sporadically around his cock did he explode inside her, reveling in the way she milked every last drop.

Lifting her up, Remy stalked toward her bedroom, keeping himself deeply rooted in her core. He was still hard as steel and was by no means finished with her. By the end of the night, he didn't want Regina to have any doubts. She belonged to him, and he was never going to let her go.

CHAPTER ELEVEN

Arienne Chevalier, or Lady Rienne as most knew her, released a pent-up breath as the driver made his way to her door. She had considered what she was about to do, but she honestly didn't see that she had much of a choice. She couldn't hire anyone to get rid of her little problem as she had attempted to do with Thierry and his nappy-headed bride. She was being watched too closely by that damnable Didier. One false move, and her little secret would be out in the open. Her options were severely handicapped.

"This is the right thing to do," she told herself again, slowly getting out of her car. It wasn't as if she was going to hurt the girl, after all. She was just going to get a little help in ending another travesty. Straightening her spine, she rang the doorbell.

"Yes, can I help you?"

Lady Rienne tried her best not to sneer at the older woman who answered the door. Hopelessly blue-collar in a floral print dress she'd probably picked up at some retail chain. The fact that the woman's skin was incredibly smooth despite her age, and that her face was practically free of lines, was something Lady Rienne deliberately ignored. The woman's salt-and-pepper hair, pulled into a bun, was thick and luxurious. The wrinkles and age spots that marked Lady Rienne's own face were noticeably absent from this woman's face—all of this was not something Lady Rienne was prepared to acknowledge. All she saw was a woman who was not fit to belong in her august family. Her dark skin gave testament to that. At least Angelique Dubois was Creole. This woman was pure Mississippi mud. Completely unacceptable.

"My name is Arienne Chevalier, but you may call me Lady Rienne. I am here to talk to you about your daughter and my grandson."

*****

"Calm down, Momma, I can barely understand you," Regina pleaded as she struggled to wake up.

Remy had ambushed her at the front door Friday night. It was now Sunday afternoon, and she'd had very little sleep all weekend. She was sore between her legs, but the small ache did nothing to dim the completeness she felt. Like she had finally come home. Despite the fact her mother was babbling about something that had her upset, Regina snuggled into Remy's side, loving the way his warm skin felt against her own. She had to smile when he kissed her forehead. She appreciated how quiet he had been, knowing she had yet to break the news to her parents. It meant a lot to her.

"Some woman came to my door talking about how you are sleeping with her lily-white grandson, and she wanted it to end! Regina, are you sleeping with some white boy? A kid? What in the world is wrong with you, girl? You can't find a man, so you're sleeping with some white woman's child?!?"

"Hell, no, I'm not sleeping with someone's child!" Regina bolted straight up in the bed. "Wait, Momma, slow down. Who told you that?"

"Some woman, Chevy, Chandelier, something crazy. She claimed you were sleeping with her grandbaby. She swore to it. She told me and your daddy you've been seeing him for months. Your father almost had a heart attack! What is going on?"

Regina felt her heart drop down to her stomach. Lady Rienne had gone to her parents. The bitch had struck at her very heart. She had been prepared for the barbs Angelique endured, but she thought Remy and his cousins had their grandmother leashed. Apparently not.

"Momma, I swear to you I am not sleeping with anyone's child."

It was technically true. Remy's parents were dead. But she was going to have to tell them about Remy sooner rather than later. She had thought she had more time to work out how she would tell them. Now she had no choice. She was going to have to tell her parents today.

"And the rest of it?" her mother demanded.

Regina sighed. "I'll be over later on today."

"Regina Belle Booker, are you sleeping with some white boy? Girl, what is wrong with you? There are plenty of single, available black men, and you had to go running off to some white boy?"

Yeah, right. If she only knew. That was actually her father speaking. No doubt Marilyn Booker was worried what her husband would think. Regina seriously doubted her mother would be all that upset if she married a blue man, as long as she got some grandbabies out of the deal. Reginald Booker, on the other hand, would have a meltdown. It couldn't be helped. Regina wasn't prepared to give Remy up. She couldn't. She'd tried that and failed miserably.

"Momma, I will be over this afternoon. We'll talk then."

She hung up quickly before her mother had a chance to ask any more questions. This was not a confession she wanted to have over the phone. Right after she hung up, Remy's cell rang.

"Yeah? Rance, I'm a little busy right... What? What the hell do you mean? When? Wasn't Thierry's spy supposed to be watching her? How the hell did this happen? Yeah, I'll meet you this afternoon. Yeah, bye."

Remy turned to her.

"I'm sorry, sweetheart." He wrapped her in his arms, rubbing her back as she melted into him. "I didn't want it to happen this way. I guess your parents won't be pleased?"

"That's saying it lightly," she murmured into his chest. "My father will probably disown me."

"Why? Because I'm white? Doesn't that make him just as bad as Lady Rienne?"

Regina pushed away from him, a little offended. Just because her father didn't believe in race mixing did not make him the black version of Lady Rienne.

"My father would not try to have you kidnapped or killed, and he damn sure never tried to control my life!"

"Doesn't he? By saying who you can and cannot date or marry? Isn't that trying to control your life?"

"It's hardly the same thing! He just wants me to be happy. He doesn't think I can truly be happy with someone who isn't black—that's just a condition of his generation. It isn't because he's racist."

"Are you sure about that, Regina?"

She wasn't, but she wasn't ready to admit it. She had hoped she could reach him. Surely, her father wasn't that pigheaded. She could reach him. She had to.

96

*****

Regina shifted in her seat as she faced her parents. Her mother, perched on the couch beside her, looked like she was about to cry. Her father scowled at her from his easy chair. This was the hardest thing she'd ever had to do. She hoped and prayed her father would understand, but that remained to be seen.

"Explain to me again why you can't find a black man? Hell, there are plenty of them out there. Your momma even tried to set you up with one. What, he wasn't good enough for you, Dr. Booker?"

She hated the way he said "Dr. Booker." It was a sneer, a curse. She had to swallow the tears that threatened to fall. She couldn't break down now; she had to be an adult.

"Daddy…"

"Don't 'Daddy' me!" Reginald thundered. "Your mother has been out there trying to set you up with someone, and you turn around and spread your legs for some white man? Do you have any idea what he really thinks about you? What he's calling you to his friends?"

"Remy wouldn't do that. He loves…"

"Loves you? Don't be a fool! He will never marry you, never treat you with respect. Why have you been sneaking around if he loves you so much?"

"He didn't want to. I asked him to. I didn't want to hurt you."

She had to make him understand. If he would just listen.

"I'm sure that's what he wants you to think," Reginald snorted. "That boy will never see you as anything other than a nigger. Free pussy at that. How could you let yourself be used like a whore? Is this what that fancy education buys? For such a so-called smart woman, you are acting like an idiot. Get out! Get out of my house."

Regina was stunned. Her father had never talked to her like that before. Her face flamed as if he had slapped her. In a way he had, using words instead of his hands. Tears fell silently down her face as she slowly got to her feet. There would be no convincing her father about Remy, not today. She felt sick to her stomach as she looked at his face. She saw hatred, not an ounce of the love she had been so sure would always be there for her. And why? Because she was in love with someone of a different race. Did that make her unacceptable as a daughter?

He wouldn't even look in her direction now. He stared straight ahead, his hands clasped on the arms of his chair in a death grip. She looked to her mother, who was crying quietly and wringing her hands together. She looked up at her, imploring.

"Break it off with this boy, Reggie," Marilyn pleaded. "Please, just break it off. Nothing good can come of this."

"I can't do that."

She had tried that, and it had only served to make her miserable. He was like an addiction, only much worse. It wasn't so much that she didn't want to live without him as much as she *couldn't* seem to live without him. She was merely going through the motions, not really living at all, when she tried to cut him out of her life. And it wasn't just the sex. They had laid in bed talking for hours this weekend, about everything. Remy was funny, insightful, open, and understanding.

And apparently way too perceptive. He had known this would happen. But Regina wasn't ready to give up just yet. These people were her parents. She could not believe that the people who gave her life, who raised her, got her through college with their own hard work, would be so closed-minded. They just had to see that times had changed.

"All I'm asking is that you give him a chance," Regina pleaded one more time. "Meet Remy, talk to him. You'll see that he's nothing like you think he is."

Her father ignored her, staring straight ahead. Her mother hung her head, shaking it. Neither one said a word. Regina felt the weight of the world pressing down on her shoulders as she walked to the door. This couldn't be the last word. She had to make them understand, one way or another.

CHAPTER TWELVE

"How serious are you about this woman, Remy? Is it worth it?"

Remy looked at his twin, *really* looked at him. Rance was agitated, but not about Lady Rienne paying a little visit to Regina's parents. Something else was irritating him. It was something about him and Regina, but Remy couldn't imagine what.

"I am very serious about Regina. Do you have a problem with that?" he challenged his brother.

Rance turned away from the gathering, but not before Remy saw the telling tightening of his jaw. Something was definitely going on with him. All the rest of them, Thierry, Aubrey, Piers and Didier, were gathered close together in Thierry's den. Rance stood by a large bay window looking out. Remy could feel pain radiating from his brother, but he couldn't imagine where it was coming from.

"Do you have a problem with it, Rance? Me and Regina being together?" Remy prodded.

He really didn't think Rance had been infected with Lady Rienne's vitriolic racism. He had fully supported Thierry when their cousin had wanted to marry Angelique. So what was up with him now?

"No."

The answer was curt and to the point, and completely unconvincing.

"How did she get past you, Didier?" Thierry cut off any further conversation. "And how in the hell did she find out where Regina's parents live?"

"I can't watch her all the time," Didier shrugged. "I can do what I can, but your grandmother is a canny old bird."

Remy reluctantly turned away from studying his brother. He would get back to it later. Right now he had to make sure his hell-bent grandmother stayed away from his woman and her parents. Regina had left earlier to go talk to her parents. She had been optimistic, but Remy didn't have her high expectations. He may not have known Mr. and Mrs. Booker, but he knew and understood people. Prejudice was like a disease, and there was no easy cure. People had forsaken their children, their parents, and others they held dear because of hatred and fear of others that were different from them.

Regina was about to find that out. He could only hope and pray that what she felt for him was stronger than her parents' hate. He couldn't go through this again. He couldn't stand not being with her, not holding her. He needed to see her face when he woke up in the morning. He needed to kiss her lips before he went to sleep at night. He wasn't sure how it had happened, but he had fallen—hard.

"She's not going to just let it go," Piers warned them all.

"Do you blame her?" Rance asked from his window. "Everything she worked her entire life for is falling down around her. Granted, Thierry was a far harder blow than my brother here, but her position in society will suffer. People will begin to question whether the Chevalier boys have a... certain predilection for a... certain kind of woman."

"Don't we?" Aubrey asked before Remy could jump down his brother's throat.

The two shared a look Remy couldn't begin to define, which pissed him off for some reason. He and his twin weren't exactly close, but Rance sharing secrets with Aubrey? And what the hell was that comment about?

"Are you saying Lady Rienne was justified?" Remy demanded. "That we should find women she deems suitable to help her save face?"

"I'm sure that's not what he meant," Thierry cut in.

"I'm not so sure," Remy threw back. "Tell me, Rance. What the hell where you trying to say?"

Rance looked as if he was about to say something, then turned back to the window.

"Nothing," he said over his shoulder.

"If you have a problem, then tell me now, to my face." Remy stalked to his brother and turned him to face him.

"I have no problem with you and Dr. Booker, Remy. I wish you all the happiness in the world."

Remy felt all his anger melt away. Rance suddenly looked tired and much older than his thirty-three years. There was still something very real bothering him, but Remy was sure it wasn't Regina's race. It certainly had something to do with him and Regina being together, but her color wasn't it.

"You can tell me, you know. Whatever it is, I'm still your brother."

Remy said the words quietly, low enough for only Rance to hear.

"You are not just my brother, Remy. You're my twin. I'm glad you finally decided to remember that," Rance answered, every bit as quiet as his brother had been. "But you can't help me on this one. No one can."

Well, that sounded ominous. Remy was as confused as ever, but that was neither here nor there right now. At this moment, he had to make sure his grandmother didn't screw up the best thing that had ever happened to him. Turning away from his brooding twin, he faced his cousins once more. He noticed Aubrey looking intently in his brother's direction, but he would deal with that later.

"I don't want that woman within a mile of Regina or her parents ever again," he told the room at large. He turned to look directly at Didier. "Can you watch her? Can you make sure she doesn't get anywhere near Regina's parents again?"

"Already on it," Didier answered. "Should have thought about it when I let you in Regina's house the other night, but I didn't think she worked that fast. She must have known about her earlier."

"Which means she has someone either watching you, Remy, or watching Regina's house," Thierry added, trying to not to laugh.

Remy knew it was probably due to their conversation earlier.

"And Didier, I need you to find out who's working for her. Who is she getting her information from, who does she have watching Regina's house?" Thierry rushed on.

"I'll distract her for a while," Piers offered. "I have the perfect thing."

Remy had no idea what that was, but he was grateful just the same. This was his family, more than his father had ever been, more than Lady Rienne could ever be. The men gathered in this room were the ones he could always depend on. He didn't know how to thank them, or his brother, who had been the first one to inform him that their grandmother had paid a little visit to his woman's parent's home.

"Thank you," he said to everyone. "I don't know... Regina means a lot to me."

It was hard to express how he felt. He felt a knot of pure emotion gathered in his throat. He couldn't express his gratitude.

"Maybe you should look into doing something more than just hanging out at night, seeing as how you're trying to be all respectable," Thierry suggested, changing the subject.

Touchy-feely emotions were never Thierry's strong point, except when Angelique was in the room. He and Rance had that bad-ass, macho man thing down to a science. It was hilarious to see him melt like butter in a hot frying pan when his wife was around. Remy could only hope Rance would mellow as well one day.

"Is it that serious?" Rance asked incredulously.

"Oh, hell yeah it is."

Remy wasn't sure where that had come from, but it was nonetheless true. He knew it was way too soon to talk to Regina about something more serious, but he was positive that this was it for him.

"I know you don't need to work," Piers began cautiously, "but I can't see you as the house husband type."

"I think I would look damned cute wearing a little apron, taking care of the kiddies," Remy quipped with his signature slow, lazy grin.

All the men looked at him in absolute shock, until a tinkling laugh filled the room.

"Why, Remy, I am sure whomever you are talking about would love nothing more." Angelique laughed as she breezed into the room, directly to Thierry's side.

"I think I feel the need to bake something," Remy said, walking out. "I'll see y'all later."

The truth was he had to get to Regina. If his guess was correct—and he was afraid it would be—she was going to need him, and he planned to be there for her.

*****

Regina toyed with her gumbo, not really interested in eating. Two weeks, and her father still refused to talk to her. She had spoken to her mother almost every day, and even seen her twice, but Marilyn Booker refused to talk about the man in her daughter's life. To her credit, the older woman never tried to get her to give Remy up. She more or less ignored the situation, dealing with more mundane things instead.

She spent all the rest of her free time with Remy. He had practically moved into her tiny house. He cooked breakfast and dinner for her daily, sometimes even bringing her a hot lunch at work. The past two weekends, they had gone out to his grand house hidden in the bayou to inspect the work that had been done over the week and add personal touches here and there. It was crazy how one part of her life was coming together, while another was completely falling apart.

Today was the first time she'd been to brunch with her friends in almost three weeks. It felt good to be able to talk to someone about the simultaneous mess and miracle her life had become. Talking to Remy about her parents usually resulted in an argument. He refused to see that her parents were nothing like Lady Rienne. Despite her father's pigheadedness, he was just worried about her. His objection was out of love; he had seen too much racism to just turn it all off. Remy refused to acknowledge that.

"He kicked you out of the house?" Katrina asked incredulously. "Did you remind him you bought that house?"

"That's not the point, Katrina," Jade broke in before Regina could answer. "You don't talk to your parents that way."

Katrina just snorted. "Maybe you and Reggie here don't. If it were me, I would be reminding that old coot exactly who paid the bills."

"You are definitely not southern," Jade muttered, shaking her head.

"And they are definitely no better than that crazy-ass Lady Rienne," Katrina shot back.

"That's not true!" Regina protested. "My dad…"

"Yeah, yeah, yeah. Old South, segregation," Katrina waved her fork around as she talked. "But what does that have to do with the here and now? You have a man who's obviously crazy about you. Your parents should want you to be happy above all else. Isn't that supposedly what parents are for?"

"You act like you don't have parents," Jade protested.

"I don't," Katrina replied blithely. "And would your parents act like Reggie's?"

"No," Jade admitted.

"Well, what can we do?" Angelique broke in to stop the bickering.

"If I can find a way to get them to see what he's like..." Regina started. "They've never even met Remy. I'm sure once they meet him..."

But Regina wasn't so sure. Remy's words had taken root in the fertile soil of doubt in her mind. Was her father holding on to the issues of the past to foster his hatred? Some people were like that, holding on to hate so that they could feel; some held on so they could remember. The human psyche was a mystery. She was scared that she had stumbled onto the ugliest part of her father's mind. She was scared things between them would never be the same, never be healed. She had always been so close to her parents. This was killing her.

If her father would not relent, Regina knew she wouldn't give up Remy. With each passing day, he was becoming more and more a part of her. She loved him. And he loved her. It wasn't something you could just walk away from.

"I can have a little dinner party," Angelique suggested, taking Regina's hand in hers. "I'll invite them myself. I can turn it into a planning session for the projects I have going right now. I won't take no for an answer; besides, your mother promised to help. I think I'll even invite Arienne. She wouldn't dare say anything in front of Didier and Thierry."

Regina smiled at Angelique's use of Lady Rienne's real name. She was the only person in the state of Louisiana who dared call the woman by her given name—and got away with it.

"That whole Didier thing is just plain weird," Jade said, pushing her salad around. "Why is the old dragon so afraid of him anyway? He's not related to her."

"He has been working for Thierry for a while, right?" Katrina asked. "He probably has dirt on the old lady. What I wouldn't give to know what that dirt is."

"Maybe you can seduce it out of him," Jade suggested. "You are our resident femme fatale. He's seriously easy on the eyes. I dare you."

"Yeah, Katrina," Angelique chimed in, her voice lowering to a conspiratorial whisper. "Didier doesn't really *work* for Thierry. Every time I bring it up, he changes the subject. I am *dying* to know what's up with that whole situation. Plus, apparently Didier is actually staying at Arienne's house! I can't see her meekly accepting that, but he's there."

"In her house? How the hell did they pull that one off?" Jade dropped her fork and stared at Angelique in absolute awe.

"That's one way to keep an eye on the old bat," Regina agreed. "How about it, Katrina? You up for seducing the mysterious Didier?"

"What am I, the group slut?" Katrina groused, pushing her chair away from the table. "Is that what you think of me?"

The other three women stopped teasing and looked at Katrina with a mixture of shock and horror. They had often joked like this; Katrina used to accept the moniker of "femme fatale" with pride. What was up with her?

"No one thinks you're a slut, Katrina," Jade cried, grabbing Katrina's hand.

"You're a sexy, assertive woman who knows what she wants," Regina assured her. "There is nothing in the world wrong with that."

"Don't play psychoanalyst with me, Regina. I don't need it," Katrina huffed, petulantly snatching her hand away from Jade's grip. "You all just sat here and asked me to seduce a man to get answers out of him. That is something you ask a whore to do."

"We were just kidding," Jade insisted.

"And that was funny?" Katrina retorted. "I don't think so."

To the other women's dismay, tears formed in Katrina's eyes. This was not the Katrina any of them were used to. Regina hadn't seen Katrina cry since their second year of college when she'd told her, in confidence, about her childhood. Katrina's mother was a stripper-turned-prostitute with a bad heroin habit. Katrina'd had it rough growing up. It had taken months of impromptu "sessions," with Regina researching online and in the library by day and working with Katrina by night, to help Katrina overcome some of the trauma. The various strip clubs and sex clubs Katrina owned, despite being a successful attorney, was part of her therapy. Unorthodox, but it worked for her. Regina had begun to hope Katrina was on the road to being able to have a normal, healthy relationship soon. When she had dated a couple of guys for longer than a month, it had been a major breakthrough. Yes, relapse was normal in any kind of recovery, but generally it didn't happen this late in the healing process. It had been eight years; Katrina shouldn't be this sensitive.

"Katrina, I swear, we didn't mean anything by it. It was a joke. Maybe a poor one, but I swear, it was just a joke," Regina assured her friend, looking directly in her eyes so the other woman could gage her sincerity.

"Hell, *I'd* seduce him," Jade muttered, picking at her salad once more.

"Yeah, you'd have to lose your virginity first there, Virgin Mary," Katrina snapped, getting to her feet and throwing some money on the table. "That should cover my part of the bill. I'm out of here. And when the hell did you start eating rabbit food, Jade?"

With that, she was gone, her normal casual stride turning into a brisk walk down the sidewalk.

"What the hell was that about?" Angelique asked no one in particular as she watched Katrina disappear down the street.

"I have no idea," Regina shook her head. "But I'd bet you dollars to donuts it wasn't about anything said here today. I for one can't wait to find out."

CHAPTER THIRTEEN

Regina woke, feeling sick to her stomach. She barely made it to the bathroom before she gave up the fabulous dinner Remy had cooked the night before. She had no doubt as to why she sick to her stomach: Today was the day of Angelique's dinner party. She had no idea how the other woman had done it—she'd not only convinced her mother to attend, but her father would be there too. It had been a month since she'd seen him. She had no idea what to expect.

"Are you okay, baby?"

She hadn't meant to wake Remy, but she wasn't surprised that she had. Remy was basically living at her house now that they were dating regularly.

"It's just nerves." She took the cold washcloth he held out to her and wiped her face before moving to the sink to thoroughly brush her teeth and rinse her mouth with a healthy dose of mouthwash.

When she looked up, she found Remy hovering over her, looking like he wanted to say something.

"What?"

"We don't have to be there for a while. I want to show you something. Are you up for it?"

She suspected he wanted to say something else, but she let it go. He would tell her when he was ready.

"Sure," she answered brightly. It might take her mind off her parents for a while.

"Good."

He looked at her again, opened his mouth, closed it again, then walked out of the bathroom.

An hour later, they were standing outside a small café in the heart of the Quarter, about a block and half away from Café Du Monde. It looked as if it had been recently remodeled, typically French, with plenty of space for several outdoor tables. Above the door and on the large picture window read *Regina's*.

"Do you like it?" Remy asked, coming behind her and wrapping his arms around her.

"It looks nice," she answered carefully. "What is it exactly?'

"It's my new restaurant. Our restaurant, actually."

That one threw her.

"Um, I think it's an excellent idea... for you. Remy, you don't expect me to..."

A peal of laughter stopped her from going any further. She couldn't help but feel relieved, if not a bit embarrassed. She had no idea where Remy saw this relationship going, but she was not about to give up her career, something she had worked so hard for, to run a restaurant.

"You honestly thought I wanted you to help me run it?' Remy laughed even harder at her guilty expression. "I love you to death, Regina Belle, but cooking and waiting tables are not among your many bountiful gifts."

"What did you say?" Regina gawked at him. Did he even realize what he had just said? Did he mean it?

"I said that cooking and waiting tables..."

"No, not that," she cut him off. "The other part."

"That I love you? Of course I love you. I've told you that before."

He looked genuinely confused, like he couldn't understand why she was shocked. Regina had to shake her head.

"In bed, maybe," she explained.

"What? It don't matter in bed, *cher*?" Remy drawled, taking her into his arms again. "That happens to be where I do my best talkin'."

"Remy, when you say something in bed, but never say it out of bed, it tends to lead one to believe it's just something you say, you know, in the heat of passion."

"I will just have to make sure to say it *out of bed* every bit as often as I say it in bed," he informed her, holding her close. "Regina, I need to ask you something."

She tried to move away, but he held her tighter.

"What is it?"

A lot of things ran through her mind, some good, some bad. She closed her eyes and held on a little tighter.

"Sweetheart, when was the last time you had a period?"

*****

Remy paced outside the bathroom door, looking at his watch again. She had been in there for twenty minutes. How long did it take for a simple pregnancy test anyway? Really, the test was more for her than it was for him. He already knew. He had known since the night it happened, when he'd had Didier break into her house. If she hadn't gotten pregnant that night, the many nights since would have surely taken care of it. There was no way in hell he was going back to wearing condoms after being bare inside her, and she had never asked. Neither of them had brought up the subject.

Would she be happy? Would she be pissed? Lord help him, he couldn't help but be inordinately happy. Regina was his everything; he didn't need any other assurances. He hoped and prayed she wouldn't feel trapped, but there had never been any chance he would let her go. The last thing he wanted to do was trap her, but he would be damned if he felt bad about this.

When the door creaked open, a visibly stunned Regina emerged. He couldn't gauge any feelings beyond shock, which immediately made him nervous. His heart was beating so hard he could feel it knocking against his rib cage. He wanted her to happy; he prayed she was happy. Lord knows he was. He felt like howling it to the moon. But without her happiness, there wasn't much of a point.

He was ecstatic that inside her womb was living, breathing proof of his love for her. To him, any child they created together was an extension of the bond they shared. He could not begin to explain it, but from the first time he'd touched her, his entire world had shifted and refocused—and the object of his focus was her. Nothing else mattered; no one else mattered. There was just Regina Belle and Remy.

"Honey, you look like you just saw a ghost." Remy attempted to lighten the mood somewhat. Maybe he should have waited to tell her what he'd already known. He had to admit, part of his reasoning was to bolster his case before the inevitable happened. Regardless of what Regina thought she could do, her father would never accept Remy, not any more than Lady Rienne would accept Regina or Angelique. Once there was a child, it was a done deal. No matter what happened tonight, God willing, there would be a permanent bond between them that no one could sever.

"Granted, this is New Orleans, so ghosts are known to abound…"

"I'm pregnant," Regina whispered in awe. "Remy, I really am pregnant."

To Remy's consternation, big, fat teardrops began to fall from her beautiful eyes. He felt as if he'd been gutted from his sternum to his gut. She wasn't happy. Did that mean she didn't care about him as much as he had believed? Had he deluded himself into thinking he could force his way into her heart? How had he misread so many things, so many indicators that she cared for him, maybe even loved him? He didn't believe he had misread her. Damn it, he *felt* it; whenever they were together, he felt the magic between them. He wasn't willing to consider it might have just been his imagination, just a passing fling. But why the hell was she so upset?

"Oh, God, Remy I never believed it would ever happen," she looked up at him, her heart swimming in her eyes. "I am really pregnant! I'm going to be a mother!"

Remy fell to his knees in absolute relief even as Regina flew into his arms. Despite his best efforts, tears welled and fell from his eyes every bit as much as from hers. It would be all right. No matter what happened tonight, or next week, or even next year, it would be all right.

*****

This was not going well. Regina cast a nervous glance at one corner, where her father and Lady Rienne huddled together in conference. Not a good sign. It was like seeing David Duke and Jesse Jackson in some kind of bizarre conspiracy. Her mother was in an opposite corner, deep in conference with Jade's mother, blithely ignoring the tension rife in the room. It was an art, really, something older southern women seemed to excel at—ignoring the elephant in the room, even as the elephant stomped everything in its path into dust. Angelique's father, Mayor Dubois (with his wife noticeably absent) was in deep conversation with Piers and Rance about something probably horribly important only to them. Didier seemed to be everywhere at once, more often than not, hovering somewhere close to Lady Rienne and Regina's father. Thierry and Angelique were nowhere to be seen, which happened fairly often at gatherings like these. Katrina was sulking in a corner, with Aubrey, of all people, by her side.

Regina couldn't help doing a double take at that sight. She could not think of two more diametrically opposed people in the world. Aubrey looked as he always did, like the professor he was; regular slacks, a tweed dinner jacket, a simple white dress shirt and a plain brown tie. Not to mention the glasses. Odd, he didn't seem to squint or look especially carefully at things, as most people with glasses were prone to do, yet Regina couldn't ever recall seeing him without them. Katrina was her flawless self in a red silk dress that complemented her reddish skin tone to perfection and hugged her generous curves. The mythical Xena didn't have crap on Katrina; the woman held herself like the goddess she was. She even had the nerve to wear two-inch heels despite her already five–foot-ten frame. It seemed like she should have dwarfed the quiet-tempered Aubrey, but she didn't.

"Now there's living proof that the end has come," Remy whispered in her ear. "The next thing you know, cats will be cozying up the dogs, bunny rabbits will only have one child, Jade will soon be having wild orgies with a coven of witches..."

"Or a Dubois will marry a Chevalier," Regina couldn't help but cut in before she dissolved into a fit of hysterical laughter. She had a feeling that might not go down so well in this crowd.

"My dear, I do believe you are right," Remy whispered with a great deal of faux shock. "I have to leave immediately and head to the nearest church. I feel a sudden need to repent. Speaking of which—" he grabbed her around the waist and ushered her out of the room into the kitchen, where he was catering the night's dinner. "I want to talk to you before we spring... anything on the gathered guests."

"You mean the baby." Regina's hand went to her stomach, rubbing reflexively. She hadn't planned on telling anyone just yet. She wanted to keep this secret knowledge just between them for now. She wanted to hold on to the happy little cocoon surrounding them for a little while longer.

"Yes and no," Remy answered, focusing on a pot of something that smelled delicious. "A damn shame to invite a body to dinner, then make them cook it," he muttered under his breath, but Regina wasn't fooled. Remy loved to cook.

"Remy, with your new restaurant, you will be working crazy hours," Regina hedged.

It just dawned on her that with the baby coming, she probably wouldn't be seeing very much of the baby's

117

father. Running a restaurant was hard work and long hours. If this was what he really wanted to do, there would have to be some adjustments.

Odd how she was thinking of things like this when, just this morning, she'd had no clear idea where any of this was heading. She had hoped, but this was new territory for her. Analyzing her own life was certainly not as easy as studying others'. In one month, she had gone from a single youngish professional to a taken pregnant lady. This was going by so fast, she barely had time to catch up.

"Actually, the restaurant will only be open for breakfast and lunch, and although I will design the menu and such, I already hired a capable head chef and manager." He answered her head on, turning to face her as he did so.

"You did this already? Before you knew?"

"Regina, I've known you were pregnant for about a week and a half. But yes, I did this before I knew, which is part of the reason I wanted to talk to you alone."

As happy as she was to hear that, she was flummoxed. So, he had made sure he would have time for her before he knew she was pregnant, but he had known she was pregnant for at least a week. Why hadn't he said anything? What was this little *tête-à-tête* about?

"Look at your face, *cher*," he laughed, softly caressing her cheek. "I can read everything you're thinking by that expressive little face of yours. I didn't tell you because I thought you would have figured it out already. When I knew you hadn't, I told you." He shrugged. "I guess I should have known, seeing as you have so much on your mind. But the restaurant..." He reached into his pocket, pulling out a small box, then pulled her flush to him. "I was thinking maybe we could move into our little house in the bayou, see how it fits." Flipping open the box with one hand, he revealed a simple solitaire. Not cheap, but understated and elegant. The diamond that was winking in the glow of the kitchen lights might not have been obscenely large, but it was the clearest, most beautiful single rock she had ever seen. It was perfect.

She couldn't really say she hadn't been expecting this moment. It had run round and round in her mind since they'd bought the pregnancy test, and every second after seeing the results. She had fully expected this to come sooner or later. Despite all of Remy's quirky devil-may-care attitude, he would want to get married since she was carrying his child. The box proved he had been thinking about this far longer than he had known about the baby. Had he asked her a week from now, she had no idea what she would have said. But he got that rock before... wait, had he gotten it before?

"Remy, when did you buy this ring?" He had said he'd known she was pregnant for about a week. Her answer would depend on his answer.

"The Monday after I broke into your house," he admitted. "I lifted a ring from your jewelry box to make sure I got the right size, and it took a little bit longer than I estimated to get the design just right, but I wanted it to be perfect for you. I wanted a ring that reflected you. Simple, elegant, classic, and timeless. I've been carrying it around for two weeks now..."

"Yes!" she cut him off. She really didn't need to hear any more. "Yes, yes, a thousand times, yes!"

CHAPTER FOURTEEN

There were times in life that called for a really good fart joke, or at the very least, a slightly off-color tease. Although Remy knew down to his bones that this was such a time, he managed to bite down on the inside if his cheek to hold the joke back. The only voice going was Angelique's, trying her best to keep everyone engaged while deftly handing out job assignments for her charity. Remy had to give it to her, she was some kind of general, first artfully finding out what a person was best suited for before handing out tasks accordingly. She was truly masterful, and Remy thoroughly appreciated the underhandedness of it all, but it did little to ease the strain boiling right underneath the surface.

Seated between Regina and her father, Remy had to restrain himself from his natural predilection for wisecracks. He instead concentrated on the interesting tableau across from him. Originally, Jade was supposed to be seated next to her parents and Katrina, but Rance had slid into the chair next to her, placing himself between Jade and her mother. Interesting, but not half as fascinating as Aubrey sliding into the chair next to Katrina. That left Thierry flanked at the head of the table by Lady Rienne and Reginald Booker. The look on Thierry's face was just priceless. Angelique was left at the other end of the table, smiling serenely as she sat in relative peace between Didier and Piers.

"What exactly is it that you do, Mr. Chevalier?" Reginald Booker snapped as he pushed his food around his plate.

Piers, Thierry, Rance, and Aubrey all looked up at the question. This time Remy did laugh. No doubt Regina would be a little peeved, but it was funny. Reginald's refusal to refer to him by name had led to this all night long. Not that he bothered to talk to him or any of the Chevalier men much. If Remy had to guess, he would bet Reginald was about to attempt to show his daughter how lazy and shiftless her fiancé was. He no doubt knew Remy was swimming in money, but Reginald would still attempt to paint him as a bored ne'er-do-well. So be it.

"Actually, I'm opening a restaurant in about a month or so," Remy answered smoothly, garnering shocked looks from his brother and Lady Rienne. Thierry had known, and Piers and Aubrey would be happy for him whatever he did. But it was nice to irritate Lady Rienne and his brother a little. Lady Rienne would be put out because running a restaurant was not an appropriate career for someone of his high bloodlines; Rance because he hadn't known. "Although I was contemplating, er, dancing for awhile."

Thierry turned bright red, and Angelique made choking noises she quickly covered by taking a drink of water. Perfect.

"Dancing?" Aubrey looked confused. "You can dance?"

"It was our Remy's poor attempt at humor," Thierry replied dryly.

"Restaurants take a lot of time," Reginald went on, still playing with his food more than eating it.

Remy was downright offended by that move. He had made a delicious shrimp and crayfish Creole, blackened catfish with his own light signature sauce,

121

saffron rice, and steamed asparagus. Maybe not exactly a five-star meal, but a decent one. There were even sweet potato biscuits, but not a single comment on the food. Ungrateful ingrates—every one of them. It was a fabulous meal; the least they could do was eat it! Next time he'd feed them gruel.

"Actually, I will be more of a director than an on-site manager or chef," Remy replied. "Something wrong with your food?"

"What?" Reginald looked genuinely perplexed.

"Your food, you haven't eaten a bite," Remy replied jovially. "I may not be the best chef in New Orleans, but I do know my way around the kitchen."

That threw good old Reginald off base, as he'd known it would. Without thinking, the man shoveled a bite into his mouth. Remy was willing to bet the man had no idea what he'd just put in his mouth, for all the attention he paid it.

"Point is, there won't be time for much else," Reginald continued after he had forced down a bite.

"I will make time," Remy assured him, unwilling to qualify the remark. He didn't want to piss Regina off. It was her call as to when and where to tell her parents about the engagement and the baby.

"Time for what?" Remy had known the question was coming, and Reginald didn't disappoint.

"We're getting married."

The last thing in the world Remy was expecting was for Regina to speak up. She looked defiant and more than just a little mad; he was just relieved she wasn't mad at him. She glared directly at her father, looking rebellious and adorable. That was his Regina Belle.

122

"Really? Oh my God, that's fantastic!" Angelique bubbled, either immune to the alarm and revulsion Reginald and Lady Rienne were emitting, or simply just ignoring it.

"Oh, baby." Marilyn wrapped her arms around her daughter, visibly excited and pleased by the news.

"Marilyn," Reginald warned, only to be ignored.

"Oh, just shut up, Reggie!" Marilyn snapped, momentarily forgetting the avid audience gathered around the table. "My baby is getting married!"

"Over my dead body!" Lady Rienne fumed, stomping to her feet. "One is bad enough, but two? Are you boys trying to bury me? After all I've sacrificed for this family, you will NOT bring another... one of *those people* into this family!"

Oh, it's about to hit the fan now, Remy thought to himself, leaning back in his chair to brace himself for the coming storm.

"See what I mean, Regina!" Reginald thundered, also rising to his feet and pointing directly at Lady Rienne. "Did you hear what that old bat thinks of you? And to hear her tell it, she raised the boy. How is he any different?"

"I think that ring on my daughter's finger makes him very different," Marilyn scolded her husband without letting her daughter out of the bear hug she had Regina in. "You can't paint everyone with the same brush."

"I forbid it, Remy Chevalier! Do you hear me?" Lady Rienne exploded. "You will not marry that woman!"

"I think you should sit down and breathe," Remy told his grandmother in a bored voice. "You sound unhinged, and your face is getting all blotchy. Of course

I'm marrying the good Dr. Booker. She has reformed me; it's my duty see her reformations through."

Maybe that was a tad bit antagonistic, but he couldn't help himself. It was just too easy.

"No, hell you won't!" Reginald shot back. "You will not marry my daughter!"

"Yes, Daddy, he will," Regina said with quiet dignity.

"Regina, if you do this I will disown you," Reginald threatened. "You will no longer be my child."

"Well, Daddy, that's too bad, because I am marrying Remy." Remy was so proud of how strong Regina's voice was. Shaking off her mother's embrace, she stood and faced him down. "I love him, with all my heart. And I know he loves me just as much. I will marry Remy, and I will be happy. I'm sorry if you can't accept that, but all you are doing is losing a daughter, not punishing me. And you are losing your grandchild as well."

And with that parting shot, Remy watched his woman walk out of the room, head held high.

"Is she... is she...?" Lady Rienne sputtered, unable to get the words out.

"Absolutely," Remy answered smoothly, standing up to follow his woman out. He was driving, after all. "Right and proper. Now, if you'll excuse me, I must take my woman home."

CHAPTER FIFTEEN

Arienne paced her study, trying to come up with a plan. This was untenable; it could not be allowed to happen. She should have expected this from Remy, but after that last slut years ago, she would have thought he had learned his lesson. Of all her grandchildren, Remy was easily the smartest, though he never showed it. And he could read people. How had he allowed himself to be caught like this a second time? Something had to be done.

Never mind what might be revealed if that child was ever born; the Chevalier name would never recover. One she could explain away as a fluke, an anomaly. Two began to look like a pattern. With Rance and Piers giving no indication of settling down any time soon, there was no example she could hold up to let others know the Chevalier family had not permanently sunk into the gutter. What would her friends say? How many were already whispering behind her back, trying to take her place as the *grande dame* of society? After all she had been through to get here, how dare her degenerate grandsons try to ruin it for her!

"Whatever you're thinking, I would strongly advice against it."

Arienne turned to face one of her last hopes. Rance.

"I haven't the faintest idea what you are talking about," Arienne breezed. "It has been a while since you deemed it necessary to visit your grandmother. To what do I owe this honor?"

"Remy."

Arienne was shocked. The last person she would expect to champion Remy was his twin. The two had been at odds since birth, as different as two people could possibly be. While Rance had never given her a minute's worry, Remy was unruly, insubordinate, and an all-around underachiever. Rance had been a straight-A student and graduated second only to Aubrey; he was now a graduate of Annapolis and Harvard Law. He had been a decorated officer, and he now ran Chevalier & Associates. There was never a whiff of scandal or rumor surrounding him. Despite his interesting peccadilloes, he knew how to keep his private life private. But then, so had Thierry, once upon a time.

"I know you, of all people, are not here to state your brother's case." Arienne shrugged off her concern, moving to sit behind her desk. It gave her an imaginary sense of superiority over her comparatively large grandsons. Silly, but she would take it. "Pour yourself a drink, it's after four."

"Thank you, no," Rance said, staying on his feet in front of her delicate antique desk.

Not a good sign.

"Well, spit it out, boy. I do not appreciate you standing here glowering at me."

Rance was silent so long that Arienne began to squirm. She hated that stare; it let on none of what he was thinking. There was only one person in the world with a stare that could unnerve her like Thierry and Rance's, and he was long gone and buried in her mind. Still, she would not show him he was getting to her. Damn grandchildren. Their fathers never gave her this kind if trouble. She was beginning to think these things must jump generations.

"That girl, Cherry, was never pregnant with Remy's child."

Arienne stiffened, looking away at the accusation there. She hadn't killed the poor slut, no matter what they might think. The woman had obviously been weak, but she had most definitely been pregnant. Arienne knew for a fact Remy had been sleeping with the low-class whore. She'd had the private investigators she'd hired take the pictures to prove it.

"I don't know what your brother told you…"

"My brother never said a word, but I know him."

"You know nothing," Arienne hissed. She was sick to death of this little brotherhood club the five of them had going on. If Thierry and Remy wanted to wander off the plantation, that was all well and good, but she would be damned if she lost any more, especially to… a certain kind of woman. "I had Remy followed, I knew he was seeing that swamp trash…"

"Remy hadn't been sleeping with Cherry for over six months. It was impossible that the child was his; she only claimed it was because Remy was her friend. She didn't know what else to do. But he never defended himself to any of us, he just took the blame for what you drove her to. I am telling you right now, *Lady* Rienne, if you raise so much as one finger to ruin this for my brother, I will personally stand next to Didier and Thierry and let loose every one of your dirty little secrets. You hear me?"

Rance, the paragon of all her grandchildren, turned on his heel and walked to the door, leaving her stunned and shaken. Then he turned around for the kill shot.

"It won't be the last, you know. Aubrey's not even trying to fight it, and I… I can't promise you I will be who you need me to be. My advice to you is to marry Piers off to some socially acceptable girl before it all hits the fan. If I can't hold on, well, I would rather see you ruined than see a tear fall from her eyes. I'm not as nice as Thierry. I will either have you committed, or expose you, I don't really care which." Shaking his head after one long look, he was gone.

The fury hit with such force that Arienne couldn't see straight. Thierry had known, but there was very little Thierry didn't know. Given the fact that he was so close to that damnable Didier, he probably knew the whole sordid story. But Rance too? Possibly even Remy. How many of her damned grandchildren knew her secret, and how long before it spilled out?

"Whatever you're thinking, don't."

"How long have you been sulking in the shadows, Didier?" Arienne demanded, wearily rubbing her forehead. "Why don't you just leave me alone?"

"Why don't you just leave them alone?"

"And let them ruin everything I have built with my own two hands?" she spat. "Do you have any idea how long it took me to get here? And they are bound and determined to tear it all down. For what? Some vague sense of love? Love is an empty promise that brings nothing but heartbreak. This is real, this is tangible!"

"To you, this is your love." Arienne hated Didier's calm rationality. "Apparently, they want something more. All the money and power, and in the end, they just want a good woman to come home to. Women who understand their needs, maybe?"

Arienne wanted to speak, but she was too infuriated to form any words.

"Get out of my office!" she screamed, uncaring if the household staff heard her raise her voice for the only time in her life. "And while you're at it, get out of my damn house!"

"I'll get out of your sight," Didier sighed, "but I won't be far. And I'm definitely not leaving your house. But then, we both know why, don't we, Lady Rienne?"

A priceless vase flew out of her hands to crash in to the wall beside the door before she could control herself. White-hot fury and ice-cold dread clashed inside her, leaving her shaking. It was going to fall apart. All of it was going to fall apart, and there was nothing she could do about it. The very people she had hoped to leave her legacy to were the ones who were destroying it all.

CHAPTER SIXTEEN

Her wedding day. Strange, but no matter how much she'd wished this day would come, she'd never really believed it would happen.

"Oh, Regina, you look so beautiful. I am so happy. Twice!"

Regina smiled at her mother as the older woman sniffled into a dainty handkerchief. Turns out, all her mother really wanted was to see her settle down and start a family. Her father, on the other hand, would not be attending. Lady Rienne was front and center, but that was only to save face.

"Hey, no thinking of the bad stuff," Katrina whispered in her ear, a sheen of tears in her eyes. "This is your day. Better you than me."

There was a sad wistfulness in Katrina's voice, but the sentiment was real.

"Thanks." Regina hugged her friend, then turned to give Jade and Angelique similar embraces.

Because she couldn't possible choose between them, she had one matron of honor and two maids of honor. Too bad they couldn't find Solange; then numbers would have been evenly matched for Remy's best men. Instead, her mother would not only be the mother of the bride, but a bridesmaid also. Angelique's father would give Regina away. All in all, it was just about as perfect as real people could hope for.

"Just remember," Jade whispered before the other women got ready to walk down the aisle, "if it was perfect, you know, with your dad and everything, the marriage would fall apart in six months. Now you are destined to be married forever, because there is discord during the nuptials."

"Jade, that is an incredibly weird thing to say," Regina laughed. "But I love you for it."

*****

Remy's heart filled to bursting as he watched his bride slowly float down the aisle. She was beautiful. The rich darkness of her skin seemed to make the white gown more ethereal. The silk clung to her gorgeous body that still refused to show evidence of his child growing there. He was going to have to fatten her up. Who would have thought it? Him and a psychiatrist?

Well, people always told me I needed therapy, Remy thought with inordinate glee. *So glad I did.*

About the Author

Shara Azod is a proud graduate of Trinity University, where she acquired her B.S. in Business Administration. She also spent four years serving in the Navy. She has traveled extensively, but her favorite destination is Paris (of course!). Bahrain, Hong Kong, and Sicily are very close favorites. She fell in love with romance novels at the age of 13 after *reading The Flame and the Flower*. Her first attempt at romance was three binders of an on-going saga featuring herself and the members of Duran Duran. She is currently married with two gorgeous children. She met her husband in Japan, they shared their first date in Hawaii, and they later married in San Diego. She's lived in Southern California, Chicago and Sicily. She currently resides in the south. Shara loves to hear from her fans, so feel free to email her anytime!

Email: shara.azod@gmail.com
Web: www.sharaazod.com

Printed in the United Kingdom
by Lightning Source UK Ltd.
136514UK00001B/74/P